# DIAMOND & LEGEND

*A Hood Love Story*

TOY

Cole Hart
SIGNATURE NOVELS

**Diamond & Legend: A Hood love Story**



Published in the United States of America.



Published by Cole Hart Signature, LLC.

**Mailing List**

**To stay up to date on new releases, plus get information on contests, sneak peeks, and more,**

***Go To The Website Below...***

**www.colehartsignature.com**

# 1

Pulling up to the club, Legend parked in the front just like always. The club didn't belong to him. However, the city and everything in it did. Getting out of the car, his size-ten Cool Gray Retro 3s touched the ground, slipping his keys into his pocket as he gave the valet a head nod followed by him strolling past the doorman. When crossed the threshold of Cloud Nine, all eyes were on him. That irritating ass siren that the DJs used went off, alerting all the strippers that some big money had entered the club. To the patrons that weren't from the area, Legend Thompson appeared to be nothing more than another black man looking for a good time tonight. Everyone else wasn't fooled by the low-key ensemble that he had on tonight. Legend stood six feet, two inches with brown skin, a short, faded haircut, and waves in a perfect circle formation. His beard was long but didn't reach his chest yet. His bowed legs gave him a distinct walk. The build of his upper body let people know that he spent time in the gym. He had on some dark-blue Levi jeans with a button-up gray Tom Ford shirt that his sister, Alannah, bought him. Legend was all for spending money on his two favorite things, which were cars, including the 2020 C-300 Mercedes-Benz Coupe he just parked outside, and Jordan sneakers. Everything else, he couldn't care less about. Legend's philosophy was it's better to look broke and be rich than look rich and be broke.

London was on stage, doing her usual set, when he walked in. She had been calling him for the last two weeks only for him to send her to voicemail. Now here he strolls his ass in here like the world revolved around him. London knew that she and Legend had agreed not to make things out to be more than they were, but she had fallen hard for him, even though she didn't want to. She tried not to focus on him and what he was doing. She had a song to get through and didn't need him to knock her off her square. She moved her eyes from where he stood and refocused her energy to her routine. Legend walked to the bar, gave the bartender a look, and waited for his drink to be made. There was a pretty good crowd in here tonight. It was a Thursday, and it looked like people were trying to get their weekend started. He walked to his usual table in the corner of the club. He was a man that needed to keep his eyes open and stay aware of his surroundings. Legend never sat with his back to the door, even when he was in familiar places just like now. It had been a long two weeks. Tonight was the first night that he could attempt to relax. There weren't any lingering issues clouding his mind. It was times like these that he was glad he had London in his corner. London wasn't his girl, but she also knew not to tell him no when he came looking for her. Sipping his Don Julio 1942, he watched London slide across the stage floor. He licked his lips as she positioned herself into a headstand, spreading her legs into a split. Oddly enough, he wasn't thinking about tasting her or even fucking her tonight. He only was here for one thing, and that was for her to put that mouth game to work.

London wasn't ugly by far. Her body was more shapely than one of those old Coca-Cola bottles. Her dark-brown skin and brown eyes were flawless, she had one thigh covered in a tattoo sleeve that looked like a rose garden to him, although he never asked her about it. She kept her weave long, eye lashes weren't obscenely long, neither were her nails. She did keep her nails with crazy colors. She told him it helped her when she played with her pussy on stage. He never denied the fact that she was a bad bitch. She just wasn't the one for him. The way he worked, he didn't have time for a woman of his own. London served her purpose with him, and that was it. She was a person to swallow his nut and a hole for him to stick his dick. He wasn't trying to be callous toward her, but a relationship of any kind wasn't in the cards when it came to them. He had explained that to her before they started messing around sexually. Judging by the way she had been calling him relentlessly the past two weeks, she had gotten caught up in her feelings. Tonight wasn't the night for that. She would see that soon enough. The song that London was dancing to ended, and she made her way over to him.

"I've been calling you. Are you going to tell me that you were that busy, that you couldn't pick up the phone not one time?"

"Evidently, you know the answer to that since I didn't pick up the phone, London," he said plainly.

He took a sip of his drink as she stood there fuming. Her being in her feelings wasn't his problem. She knew what she signed up for. It wasn't his problem that she did the one thing he told her not to.

"Legend, I was only calling to say hi and see how you were doing," she lied.

He knew she was lying, but he wasn't emotionally tied to her, so there was no need to point that out to her.

"You called all those times, didn't leave a voicemail, and you're looking at me now. You still didn't say hey or ask me how I was. Your sweaty ass waltzed over here talking all fast at the lip like I owe your ass an explanation. Go take a shower and meet me in the room, London, before I hurt your fucking feelings.'

"Is that the only reason you came here?"

He looked at her like she had lost her mind.

"I'm gonna go in the room. If you're not in there in twenty

minutes cleaned up and ready to suck some dick, forget you know me."

He got up and walked to the champagne room, leaving London to decide what she was going to do. She watched as he walked to the champagne room. She knew that she was being watched by the other dancers ready to take her spot, so she went to take a shower and change her clothes. When she walked into the locker room, she was met with the usual whispers, rolling eyes, and looks of disgust. This had been the norm since she was the chosen one when it came to Legend. Everyone knew that Legend's money and dick were long. However, he wasn't known to pass either out randomly. London knew that, so she wasn't going to turn down even the minimal attention from Legend. London felt that if she was around when he needed her, then she would eventually be the one to be on his arm and in his bed, not just on his dick. In the shower, she quickly washed herself because Legend was known to leave if she took too long. She could tell by looking at him that he was agitated, so she knew her window was small with him. After washing her body twice, she gave herself the final rinse and headed to the locker room naked and still dripping. Being a stripper, there wasn't a shy woman in the room. It was normal to walk around naked, wet or dry. When she got to her locker, she took her towel out to dry her body off. She was growing irritated with all the whispers going on around her. Once she was dry, she took out the outfit that she was planning to wear for the rest of the night. She slammed her locker door to let the other strippers know she wasn't for their shit tonight.

"Let me go see what Legend has planned for me tonight. I'll see y'all bitter hoes tomorrow," London said as she walked out of the locker room. She couldn't wait for the day that Legend took her out of this place. She never planned on stripping all of her life. She just wanted to snag a baller and make him fall in love. As she made it to the door of the champagne room, she realized that she wasn't confident that she had succeeded in doing either of those things.

Legend was checking his phone to see if the designer had responded to his message yet, which she hadn't. It was lightweight pissing him off that she hadn't responded in two fucking days. Since she was the one that Alannah talked his ear off about, she was the one that would do this project for him. It didn't matter; If he had to use other ways of contacting her, then he would. He didn't want to scare the damn woman, but time was getting tight. He could tell that she was an up-and-coming designer, but she needed to learn some fucking customer service and answer her damn messages. Just when he was about to send her a message to let her know how displeased he was about her not responding to his messages, London walked through the door. He looked at her walk across the floor. He was confused at why she was doing this slow motion walk with a look of constipation on her face. He knew if he laughed, there would be a one-sided argument. He didn't have the patience for all that tonight. The mission for tonight was to get a nut and go the fuck home. Not wanting to look her in face, he decided to continue to scroll through the designer's posts.

"Are you going to look at your phone the whole time? I thought you came to see me."

"Stop fucking playing with me. I came to get a nut. Going through my phone isn't stopping you from getting on your knees and putting my dick in your mouth. Either you're gonna do it, or not. Let me know so I can go home if not," he said, not bothering to look at her.

He wanted to call her out when he heard her kiss her teeth, then get on her knees. She unzipped his pants and took his dick out. She was pissed that he wasn't paying her any attention. Moments ago, here she was flexing in front of the other strippers in the locker room, and now she was fighting back the tears as she attempted to suck the soul out of Legend. Legend, on the other hand, was more concerned about the designer chick than he was about getting the blow job that he came for. Social media was never his thing, but right now, he was consumed with finding more pictures of the pretty interior designer. After going through most of her pictures, he didn't see one man in any of them. That told Legend that she was either single or her man wasn't a social media person either. He could feel the difference in the way that London was sucking him off. She was starting to do more in order to get his attention. He ran his free hand over the top of her wig. London's natural hair was down to the middle of her back. However, you could never tell due to all the fake hair she wore most of the time. Legend had learned the hard way when he attempted to grip her hair one night and the whole damn wig came off in his hands. Vowing to never do that again, he chose to run his hand over the top of her head, similar to the way someone would pet a dog.

"Catch it all," he groaned.

Doing as she was told, she swallowed all of his kids. Legend could never be too sure, so he passed her one of the complimentary water bottles for her to drink. He had seen it too many times where a stripper looking for a come up would catch a man slipping and get pregnant by them. Legend would never allow that to happen.

"Open," he told her.

London rolled her eyes but opened her mouth anyway to let him see that she had indeed swallowed his kids and the water. She felt less than a woman right now, but Legend has been this way since they started fucking around. There were nights he would remove the condom in her face, wrap it in a napkin just to flush the napkin and the condom down the toilet. In London's eyes, he was doing too much because she didn't want any kids ever. She had told him this on more than three occasions. His response was always the same. *You may not want them now, but that shit will change just like everything else.*

"Am I leaving with you tonight?" London asked.

"Is your car in the shop or something?" Legend asked.

"No. I was just wondering if we were going to spend more time together."

"When have we ever spent time together? This is the one thing I thought you understood. We're not a couple, and we never will be."

"It's been a while since we started this. I thought that maybe you would want to take this a step further."

"A step further than what, London? There ain't shit else for us to do but fuck. We do that just fine, so leave it like it is. Whenever you start talking, shit gets fucked up. If you're not moaning, calling me daddy, or saying 'right there', you don't have to speak."

"You're just rude and an asshole, do you know that?"

London was tired of Legend, but she was also torn because she felt she had earned her place as his woman. If he wasn't so damn stubborn about shit, he would see that she was all that he needed. However, she didn't want to push him away either. He did more for her just by being around her, even if it was for fucking. Legend had his mind set on being single, doing whatever he wanted with whoever he wanted. In the meantime, London had her mind set on causing any woman that was a threat to her place in Legend's life a hard time until they took their asses on to the next baller.

"You knew that shit before I fucked you."

Legend walked out without even giving London a second look. Every time he did this, she would be depressed for at least a day. It was a toxic cycle that no one knew was happening. How could they when you have London telling all the girls at the club that she and Legend are way more than they ever will be? Legend heard the rumors, but he would never confirm or deny to anyone, because it wasn't their business in the first place. London's phone rang. She picked it up, trying to hide how she really felt.

"Hello?"

"London, I'm surprised you answered the phone. Where's your boo?" one of the girls from the club asked.

"He just left. I know you saw him walk out of the club. That's why I can't stand half of y'all in here now. All y'all do is be messy and talk about each other. I'm still here in the champagne room, trying to get my head together before I go out here to make some more money."

"I was just checking to see if you were still here. There's no need for you to get all snappy with me because he left your ass in this damn club, again. I thought y'all were working on something solid. What happened to all that?"

London rolled her eyes took a deep breath and let the lies start rolling freely. The toxic cycle continued and would always be in place until Legend put a stop to it.

# 2

The keys jiggled loudly as Diamond sat on her couch watching the doorknob turn. Jakari hadn't bothered to come home for the last two days, and Diamond was over him and all his bullshit. The first night, she was worried, even calling the local jails and hospitals to make sure he wasn't hurt. When Diamond realized that he wasn't hurt but out in the streets doing something he had no business doing, her worry turned to anger. It was the anger that drove her to pack up all his shit and set it by the front door.

She had been with Jakari long enough to know that he wouldn't take her seriously when she told him to get out. He would plead his case, then try to use that dumbass manipulation to persuade her to allow him to stay, again. After being with Jakari beyond a child that he made while they were together and the numerous jobs he had lost, Diamond was tired and fed up. This was the last straw. Jakari had no idea of what he was walking into. Diamond had her Glock that she named Ethan Hawk sitting on her lap while she drank from the bottle of Patrón. The lights were off, so when she heard Jakari curse from hitting his foot on one of the boxes, she turned the light on to get this party started.

"Oh shit, D. What the hell are you sitting in the dark for? Why are all these boxes sitting in the middle of the floor?" Jakari asked.

"Niggas," Diamond said before taking another drink from the Patrón bottle.

"So you just said fuck a glass and a chaser, huh? Whose boxes are these?"

"Yours," she said, looking at him.

"Come again. What did you say?"

"The boxes are yours, Jakari. Give me my key, get your boxes, and get the fuck out," she told him.

Diamond stood to her feet, showing Jakari that she was dressed in all black. Diamond was a stacked female on the thicker side of slim thick with dark, flawless skin, plump lips, and high cheekbones that were shown off by the short haircut she rocked. At the age of thirty, Diamond gave some twenty-two-year-olds a run for their money. Jakari didn't know if she was calm because of her drinking or if she was calm because she wanted to kill him. He knew that staying out for two days would most definitely start an argument when he got home, but he never thought she would try to put him out.

"D, let me explain where I was. I got hemmed up with those niggas downtown, and the police came through arresting everyone in the house. They finally listened to what I was saying, and they let me go. You know I don't have anything to do with that street shit."

Diamond lifted her gun and shot Jakari in his kneecap. He dropped to the floor, groaning in pain. Jakari was built similar to the rapper Snoop Dogg. The only differences were he was only six feet and he didn't have the long hair. There was very little meat to protect his knee from the bullet.

"I can't believe you shot me!"

"I can't believe that you walked your black ass in here after two days, and that's the lie you came up with. I called all the jails and hospitals, Jakari. Your ass wasn't at any of them at no time in the last forty-eight hours. You really think that I'm that gone off your inconsistent dick game? It can't be the mouth that has me hooked. Lord knows you eat pussy like you're trying to eat beef jerky with no teeth in your mouth."

"Call a fucking ambulance, Diamond!" he yelled.

"I'm good on that, Jakari. You couldn't use the phone to call me, and I'm not using my phone to call the ambulance. The way I see it, that's a fair exchange. Is it not?"

"You crazy bitch. I could die if you don't call the ambulance. Call the fucking ambulance now, Diamond. This shit is serious," Jakari said with tears covering his face.

"Poor thing. Are you crying?" Diamond asked as she stood over him. "Imagine that. Big bad Jakari crying over a flesh wound."

"You shot me in my damn knee. This isn't a flesh wound. What the fuck is wrong with your crazy ass?"

"You took my kindness for weakness. You never stopped running the fucking streets, even though you know it hurts me. I think it's crazy that you can play with a woman's heart and not think that everything you do will catch up with you. But by all means, continue to project your stupid ass actions onto me. Niggas like you think they can do whatever, and a woman is supposed to stick by you because they were all just mistakes. Every time you cheated, failed to come home at night, made a baby with someone other than me, and all that other fuck boy shit you've been doing that I never heard about. All that is over. Get up and get out of my damn place. Leave my keys. If you don't, the locks will get changed I promise. You may not believe me, but I can show you better than I can tell you."

Diamond grabbed her bottle and left Jakari on the floor leaking. He lay there in pain, wondering how he came to this spot right now. Everything that Diamond said was true, especially the part about him believing that she would never leave him, regardless of what type of foolishness he took part in. Diamond left Jakari alone, not caring if he lived or died. Her love for him made her hope that he would finally realize that he will never be the boyfriend or man that she needed. It took some time, but Diamond was finally ready to be brutally honest about the relationship they were in. Jakari only wanted to hold on to her because he knew how broken she is. While everyone was out here looking for the baddest or a boss bitch, Jakari wanted a battered, bruised, and broken bitch. Those were the ones that stayed with a no-good man because they felt that they weren't going to be able to catch the eye of another man. All of which are things that he had been doing this since they started dating. This time, he had caught the diamond in the rough and lost her due to a lack of appreciation and respect. Diamond could see now that she was the prize, and it was time for her to be treated like one, no matter how much it took her out of her comfort zone. Although Jakari was a dog and a user throughout their relationship, she was familiar with him.

Diamond appeared to be a boss to the outside world. Her interior design company had taken off with the help of social media. She was making money and was too busy to wonder what Jakari was doing when she wasn't around. The one thing that he didn't think about was what would happen when she gets to the point of being fed up with him and all his bullshit. While she's standing in the hallway, she could hear him fumble around on the floor, looking for his cell phone that dropped when she shot him. Calling the cops wasn't what she expected him to do, even if he is a fuck boy. Diamond was sure that he wouldn't just call anybody, because there were times she'd heard his friends tell him how much of a good catch Diamond was for him. If he called anyone, it would be someone that would keep the fact that Diamond is the one that shot him on the low. She knows that he doesn't need the hood putting him on blast for Diamond's reaction to the constant pushing he had done to her over the years. Although it was clear to her that he was in pain and now homeless, she hoped that he understood her reasoning for shooting him. He had finally pushed her too damn far.

Diamond knows that Jakari was cocky enough to think he was going to give her a couple of weeks before he tried to come talk to her again. Everyone knew that losing Diamond was not something he was prepared to do. She finally heard the phone dialing what she assumed was his best friend's number. When she heard him pick up, she realized the phone was on speaker. She smiled as she thought about him being in so much pain that he couldn't pick up the phone like he normally would.

"I just dropped your ass off. Don't tell me y'all are arguing and shit already," Tony said.

"She shot me. I need you to come get me. I can't go to the hospital. I can't have her getting in trouble behind this," he groaned.

"Diamond shot you? Where did she shoot you?"

"She shot me in the knee, man. Are you coming or what?"

"Watch your tone. I can go back in the house and let your ass bleed out on the damn floor. I'm coming, nigga. Don't run off. I'm right around the corner, so try not to die in the next six minutes."

As she heard the call ending, she peeked around the corner to see Jakari slide across the floor, reaching for one of the boxes. He opened the box, pulling out one of his shirts. Wrapping the shirt around his knee and tying it in a tight knot to help slow down the bleeding, he bit down on his bottom lip, refusing to yell out as the pain hit him.

Now that Diamond was satisfied that Jakari had called for help and not the police, she left him in the living room bleeding all over her hardwood floors, The first thing Diamond did when she got to her room was get on the phone with her best friend to fill her in on what just happened.

"Friend, I know you're lying to me. That asshole is not in your house bleeding while you're on the phone with me. When the hell did you become so damn ruthless? You know when he dies in your house, you're gonna have to explain that shit. Claiming insanity isn't going to work." Ashera laughed.

Ashera and Diamond have been friends forever. Believe it or not, Ashera was the over the top one. Diamond was known to be calm, blunt, and very determined. Diamond knows that Ashera never thought she would get tired of Jakari's bullshit, but Ashera would be happy as hell that she did. She couldn't stop laughing at the fact that Diamond left that man to fend for himself. It tickled her that her friend was so calm while telling her the story.

"I'm not going to claim insanity, because his ass is too much like the devil to die," Diamond replied with a laugh.

Diamond heard her door open and close. She wanted to go see if Jakari had someone to get him, but she didn't want to go in there and they still be there. She kept talking to Ashera until Ashera had to get off the phone. Diamond chose that time to go see if Jakari was gone. When she walked into the living room with her bat in her hand, she saw that Jakari and a few of the boxes were gone. There was a trail of blood that she had to get up, but she would happily clean that up if she never saw his no-good ass again.

# 3

Alannah was relaxing on her brother's couch. Today was one of her off days with no studying to do, so she was doing what had become her habit—scrolling the Instagram timeline of Diamond Designs. She had run across the page by mistake and fell in love with the way Diamond put modern, abstract, and traditional pieces and designs together in a way that you had to fall in love with the space. Diamond Designs was black owned, and she only used black businesses and artists in her designs. Throughout the last year, Alannah had been exposed to numerous small black owned businesses that she never knew existed. She was amazed that there was a black-owned business for everything from rugs to house paint. For every design that Diamond did, she put the links of all the businesses that she used in the comment section. Alannah was impressed by Diamond always playing it forward. Some of the companies had shouted Diamond out because she never asked for a discount for their services, and she always brought them more business just by posting their links and contact information.

"What are you doing? I'm surprised you're not studying," Legend said as he walked into the living room in a pair of basketball shorts and slides.

"I only have one more class's final exam to worry about. The class isn't as bad as other students made it out to be, so I don't have to go overboard with studying. I'll be so glad when I'm finally finished. Graduation is only a few weeks away. I'm just looking at some new posts that Diamond Designs put up last night. She is dope as hell at what she does."

"You get all excited and shit when you talk about her designs and shit. Maybe you should look into doing that," Legend suggested.

"I know my limits, Legend. Her designs are just something that I like to look at. Put me in front of a computer, I'll be at home and happy. I just like her work. There's nothing wrong with that."

"You're right about that. How the hell do you get in contact with her? I've been trying to link up with her so she could do my man cave, but she hasn't hit me back yet."

Legend was pissed that he had messaged Diamond a week and a half ago, but she hasn't looked at the damn message yet. He could see that she was working, but she can't be that damn busy.

"You mean to tell me that a woman didn't drop everything to see what the great Legend wanted with them?" Alannah joked.

"Fuck you, okay. I'm just saying. Ol' girl's designs are fire, but her customer service skills suck ass. That's the main problem with black-owned businesses nowadays. I think they all should take a customer service course before they're allowed to operate. It's bogus as hell to ignore messages of potential paying customers. What if I go out here and get another designer to do my space? Then y'all women will be putting me on blast for not patronizing a black-owned business."

Alannah was enjoying this side of Legend. He's always the one in control of everything. Patience is something that he'll never have, and it was showing loud and clear right now. She was the only one that could laugh at Legend's frustration, and she was doing that at the moment. Legend shook his head at the way his sister was finding amusement in his anger toward her favorite Instagram designer. If she was anyone else, he would've knocked her out by now.

"You sound a little salty about all of this, bro. I promise it'll be fine if you get someone else to do your room," Alannah reasoned.

Alannah was the exact replica of their deceased mother, Marcel. She was shorter than Legend, only reaching five feet, four inches, skinny, brown skinned with brown hair that reached the middle of her back. Legend gave her a head nod instead of continuing to lie to Alannah. There wasn't a room that he wanted Diamond to design. It was an entire house. The house was supposed to be a gift to Alannah for her completing her bachelor's degree and getting a job with the government in her field of cyber security. It was supposed to be a surprise for her, but if Diamond didn't get in contact with him by next week, he was going to have to find someone else for sure. He didn't want to, but he would have no other choice.

"I might have to, but that will be a last resort. If she knows what's good for her, she'll check her funky ass messages. I have to go to Cali for a few days. Are you going to be good here by yourself?" Legend asked.

He hated leaving her alone. It didn't matter to him that she was twenty-four years old. She was and will always be his little sister.

"I'm always good. Everyone knows not to mess with me," Alannah said as she put up her fists like she was about to box someone.

Legend laughed at his sister. She did know how to box due to all the boxing, jujitsu, and women's self-defense classes he had enrolled her in. She was also a concealed weapon holder. They went to the shooting range twice a week. He made sure that, even though she was female, she could handle herself if she needed to.

"I get it, but I hate leaving you when I'm on the other side of the country. I'll have a few of the guys keeping an eye on you, but they aren't me. They know if they let anything happen to you, I'll do ten times worse to them."

"When are you gonna stop trying to be Tony Montana, bro? You've been doing this shit long enough. It's time for you to get a woman and give me some nieces and nephews to corrupt."

"Never that. I don't need any kids or a woman to spend all the money I've saved."

"That's why you find one with money of her own," Alannah countered.

"All the women on their own money shit are also the ones on that 'I don't need a man' shit. They only want a man for some dick, but now that some motherfucker has invented that damn rose thing that all y'all females use, they don't want the dick either, especially if it's attached to a man."

"Tell me why you're mad, bro," Alannah said, laughing.

"I'm not mad. I still get mine, but it's just the point. The world has these females' heads so messed up that they feel like a man is their equal. The shit is bogus as fuck. If I get a woman, she's gonna understand that I'm the head of the relationship. I'm not gonna abuse her or no shit like that, but she needs to know that I run shit," Legend said proudly.

"That's the bullshit that all you men say. A woman has no problem with allowing a man to lead. The problem comes in when leading turns into control. Telling a woman when to come and go has nothing to do with leading the relationship."

"Nobody is trying to control a chick like that. However, if she has some friends that are on some bullshit or are low-key hating her, the man she's involved with should say something to her about it. A lot of times, other people can see shit that you can't. You shouldn't just write off what he has to say. If anyone has your best interest at heart, it's the nigga you're fucking."

"I'm not about to debate this with you. Get you a woman and debate it with her," Alannah joked.

"You like telling me to get a woman. I don't need a woman, because that means I'll have two women to take care of."

"I guess you need to get one that has her own then, huh? I'm telling you that there are some hotties out here that have their own bag and aren't concerned about yours."

"That's what you say. I haven't met a female yet that isn't turned on by knowing who I am and the clout I have out here. London's silly ass still thinks she has a chance to get closer to me, and it's been a long ass time since we started fucking around. No matter how many times I tell her that ain't shit happening with us, she still thinks she has a chance."

"I just told you that there are boss ass females out here, and the first person you think of is London. The career stripper of the year. Are you serious right now? Everybody knows that you and London are nothing more than a fuck, except London. I told you when y'all started kicking it that her ass was slow as hell. She's a very pretty girl, but she ain't that smart," Alannah said as she shook her head.

The doorbell chimed. Legend went to answer it. He was waiting on Justin to come over so they could talk about this meeting they were going to have in California. Legend was feeling antsy about the meeting because it was a spur of the moment thing. If there was anything that he's learned over the years is that his supplier, Carlito Palermo, didn't do spur of the moment for anything. When he got the call yesterday, the hairs on the back of his neck stood up. Something was off, and he reached out to Justin to try to find out what the real deal was. He wasn't going to walk into anything blind if he could help it.

"What up? What up? Please tell me that one of y'all cooked. My black ass is hungrier than a hostage," Justin said.

Justin was just over six feet with wild curly hair and a few tattoos on both arms. He reminded people of the actor that played Aquaman. People thought he was from one of the islands in the Pacific Ocean, but he was born and raised in Baltimore. His mother was black, and he was told that his father was a soldier from Hawaii. Justin never met the man and didn't talk about him much.

"You stay coming over here hungry. A normal person would stop and get a bucket of chicken at least if they're already hungry. Chicken is universal. Everyone eats it," Alannah joked.

"Nah, lil' sis. Why would I spend money when I know there's a chance that one of y'all cooked already? That doesn't make sense to me. No need to spend money unnecessarily," Justin replied.

"You two are the cheapest ballers I've ever seen," Alannah said.

"On some real shit, we learned from a billionaire that the best way to stay a billionaire is not to spend money like you have it. Think about it. Do you see Bill Gates and that cat that owns Amazon with designer clothes and shit? They have big houses, cars, and shit like that. I haven't seen a real billionaire dripping in yellow diamonds and shit like those rap niggas be doing. Pay attention, sis. I'm telling you some good shit," Justin replied.

"Come on, man, so we can get this conversation out of the way. I know whatever you have to tell me will piss me off, so we might as well get it over with," Legend told him before leading him to his office.

When they got in the office, both of them took their seats. Legend knew by the look on Justin's face that shit was about to go left.

"What's the deal?" Legend asked.

"Carlito's talking, and word is, he's talking about you," Justin told Legend.

Legend shook his head because he was right. Shit wasn't just going to go left it was about to hit the damn fan.

# 4

After Justin left Legend's house, Legend sat in his office angry to the point that he wanted to physically fight somebody; it didn't matter who. He couldn't believe that Carlito would turn State's evidence, and to add insult to injury, he was setting Legend up to take the fall for everything. Carlito has been Legend's supplier since he and Justin decided to push weight only. Legend had grown tired of always dealing with the know-it-all corner boys and the bullshit that comes with street-level dealing. Pushing only weight meant that they would only deal with one person, it was up to that person to distribute everything. Now that they were dealing weight, it took some time, but eventually, they had the south side sewed up. There wasn't anything being sold that didn't come from them. Now that weed is getting legalized, Legend was in the beginning stages of opening a dispensary. He wanted some of that legal weed money. He never would've thought that weed would be legalized or that Carlito Palermo would be talking to the feds and the DEA.

Legend and Justin met Carlito when they were in their early twenties. He had been hearing about all the moves they had been making and requested to meet them. After the first meeting, Carlito kept his eye on them, watching how they moved. He eventually took them under his wing and guided them to be the men they are today. He not only taught them the drug game, but he also taught them how to move like men with money and power. Legend had to find a way to get through the meeting in Cali without tipping off the fact that he suspects Carlito is a rat. That was going to be hard as hell for both of them to do. Legend and Justin have been there in the past when Carlito killed men that he thought would talk if the heat was getting too hot. *You never leave the weakest link in the chain. It must be removed, or it will cause the whole chain to be worthless.* Legend sipped his glass of Don Julio 1942 as he reminisced about all the lessons that Carlito has taught them. Legend was having an internal battle with himself. He didn't know if he was supposed to try to forget all the things he had learned from Carlito because he could be a rat. How could he look Carlito in his face and not beat his ass? Giving any information to any authority, regardless of how big or small it was, is a violation of the street code.

Legend's phone started going off, which got his attention. When he picked it up, he saw that there was a message from Diamond Designs. This is what he needed to get his mind off the fact that the man he looked up to was nothing more than a fucking snitch.

***Diamond Designs:*** *I would like to apologize for the delay in my return message. If you are still in need of my services, just let me know.*

***Me:*** *Can you meet me tonight?*

***Diamond Designs:*** *Sure I can meet you. When and where?*

***Me:*** *Meet me at Vice at seven. When you get there, just let them know you're there to meet Mr. Thompson.*

***Diamond Designs:*** *I will do that. Is there a dress code for Vice? I know it's hard to get a reservation.*

***Me:*** *Nah. Just wear what you're comfortable in.*

***Diamond Designs:*** *Okay, I will see you then. I would like to apologize again for my how long it took me to respond to your message on my business page.*

***Me:*** *Cool.*

Things weren't cool, but Legend didn't want to tip her off to that yet. He wanted to see her face when he told her how he really felt. He thought about taking it easy on her because there could've been something wrong with her or her family. He decided he was going to allow her to explain before he went in on her. Looking at his watch, he had a few hours before it was time to meet Diamond Designs. He decided he wanted to take a nap. He might need the energy.

Diamond wasn't nervous about meeting this new potential client at first. She made the mistake of telling Ashera who she was meeting. Once she told Ashera the person's Instagram name, she started yelling and screaming in Diamond's ear. Diamond thought she had told Ashera she was going to meet a famous rapper or an athlete. She almost cursed Ashera out when she told her he was a hood celebrity of some kind. Diamond didn't care if he was President Obama; she just wanted to get hired, do a damn good job, get her money, and take her ass home.

Standing outside of Vice, she almost turned around. One thing stopped her from turning around, and that was the unknown. Diamond didn't know just how big the job was or if it would lead to other big jobs. She knew that word of mouth is the best form of advertising, and she needed the word to be spread about her and her company. If this guy was as rich as Ashera said he was, he surely had some rich friends. After taking a deep breath, she walked inside of the building. The inside of the restaurant was breathtaking. The waterfalls and koi pond added to the ambiance of the place. It was beautiful. Diamond understood why this place was so hard to get into already, and she hadn't even been seated yet.

"Welcome to Vice. How can I help you?" the young girl asked.

"Good evening. I'm here to meet with Mr. Thompson," Diamond said.

The young girl smiled and spoke into her mouthpiece. A few seconds later, a middle-aged man came to the desk.

"Good evening, ma'am. I will take you to Mr. Thompson's table. He's awaiting your arrival."

Diamond followed the gentleman through the restaurant. She caught a glimpse of what she thought was Jakari's face, but there was no way that he was in here the same time she was. *The Lord's sense of humor is not that toxic,* she thought to herself. When she got to the table that the gentleman had stopped at, she wanted to run out of the restaurant. There is no way that this man had reached out to her of all people for her services. She was sure that he had a woman somewhere that could decorate whatever he needed. Her escort pulled out her chair as Legend stood to his feet waiting for her to sit down. *So he's fine and a gentleman*, she thought to herself.

"It's nice to meet you. I'm Diamond, the owner and operator of Diamond Designs. Can I ask what type of service do you need? I know you need something decorated, but what exactly is what I'm asking?" Diamond said.

"I'm Legend. I bought my sister a house as a gift for her graduation and her getting a job in her field. She is always looking at your stuff on Instagram. That's what made me reach out to you," Legend said as he sipped his water.

Diamond looked around for the waitress or waiter to come take her order. Usually, they were at the table before she could sit down good. Here it is, she's been at the table for over five minutes, and no one has approached the table. Diamond was getting a little hot sitting at the table with Legend, so she needed something to drink immediately. She poured some water in her glass from the pitcher on the table. She hoped that it would cool her down. The last thing she wanted to do was start sweating while she talked to this man.

"Did you tell the waiter or waitress not to come to the table? I would like to order," Diamond said.

"I ordered for us both already. The food should be out shortly," Legend said calmly.

"Excuse me? You did what?"

"I ordered for us. I figured since you're too busy to respond to messages promptly, you would be appreciative of the fact that I ordered for you. That way, you wouldn't have to waste time deciding what to eat," Legend told her.

He knew that she was two seconds away from coming across the table, but she was trying to keep her anger in check. Diamond cleared her throat before folding the cloth napkin that was on the table. Legend noticed that she needed to do something with her hands to keep herself from going off on him.

"Which room in the house would you like for me to decorate?" Diamond asked.

"All of them," Legend said as he looked into her eyes.

"The entire house?"

"Yup. I don't want a room of that house not to have your touch."

"I usually charge by the room. I've never done a whole house before."

"There's a first time for everything. I'll tell you what—" Legend started to say but was interrupted by a man standing at the table.

"You put my ass out and shoot me just to be sitting up here with some nigga. I should fuck you up right now for playing in my face. This shit ain't cool, Diamond," Jakari said.

Legend put his hand up so Diamond wouldn't open her mouth. To her surprise, she swallowed what she was going to say easily. There was a commanding presence that Legend had. Diamond hoped that she wasn't the only one that felt it when he was around. She had a feeling that Jakari was about to wish that he never came over to the table at all.

"Did your fat ass mama teach you manners? You come over

here, interrupting our conversation, just to say some bullshit that you should've kept to yourself. On top of that, you threaten her in front of me as if I'm some lame motherfucker. I know you know exactly who I am and how I give it up. My question to you is which one of us should slap the piss out of you for your rude interruption? You need to go back over there with that old hoe you were eating with," Legend said.

"Nah, I want to know if this nigga is the reason you put me out and broke my heart," Jakari pleaded.

Before Diamond could respond, Jakari was getting hit in the face with the pitcher of water. Jakari bent over with his hand on his face. Legend slammed his face into the table.

"It's motherfuckers like you that make me show a side of me that I hate for beautiful ladies to see. Disrespect is one thing I don't tolerate. The other thing is niggas putting their hands on beautiful women. I suggest you forget all about Diamond, homie. I want to hear you threaten me like you just did her. Tell me that you should fuck me up. I can't hear you," Legend said as he kept pressing Jakari's head to the table. Legend wasn't having this young cat coming over here interrupting them or throwing threats like shit was sweet.

Diamond was stuck with her mouth open as she watched this man she just met essentially break down the man that she used to care about. A small piece of her wanted to stop Legend from abusing Jakari, but she knew not to interfere. Jakari had no business approaching her in the first place. Jakari knew damn well why Diamond put his ass out. Him coming over here causing a scene was just for show. Unfortunately for him, he was the center of attention as he was getting broken down by Legend right now.

"Umm, Mr. Legend, these people are going to call the police on you. Please don't make this more than what it is. Jakari is not worth any charges that these people are going to try to pin on you. Please let him go. Not for him, but for you. This is not anything that you need to deal with."

Legend was going to blow this nigga's head open on this table in this packed upscale restaurant until he heard her voice. When she talked, she calmed him down somewhat. He was still mad, but he could save the killing of Jakari for another day. Hearing her tell him to stop not because of her care for the asshole that was going to die, but for him as a man made Legend stop what he was about to do. Legend got close to Jakari, then bent over to tell him something that Diamond didn't need to hear.

"You need to go home, call your mom, and tell her to make sure your insurance is paid up. You can run, but you can't hide, nigga. Your day is coming. I promise you that. Leave and do not look Diamond's way."

He stepped back from the table, allowing Jakari to stand up. Jakari could feel Legend staring a hole through him, which made him limp away in the opposite direction of where Diamond was sitting. Legend looked around for a free server. When one walked up to him, he reached his hand out for Diamond to take it and stand to her feet.

"We need another table so we can finish our meeting. Try to put us in one of those rooms in the back this time."

"Right away, Mr. Thompson."

Diamond was on edge, expecting the police to come rushing in and put Legend in handcuffs. She noticed how calm Legend was with his head held high as if he owned the place.

"You own this restaurant?" she said, sounding more like a statement than a question.

Legend smiled, showing his perfect white teeth. He didn't want her to know that he owned Vice. It wasn't common knowledge. Even the paperwork had his deceased father's name on it. Legend went to great lengths to cover his tracks in the purchase of the restaurant. Only a person looking for him would find him after looking hard.

"If I answer that truthfully, do you promise not to tell Alannah?" he asked.

"I don't know her, so how could I tell her anything?" Diamond asked.

"You don't know her yet. When you do get to know her, you can't tell her, but yeah, I own this place. What gave it away?" he asked with a smile.

"You're so calm for a person that just slammed a man's face into the table. On top of that, you're still giving out orders like you can do that. I use my context clues at all times," Diamond said with a giggle.

"Context clues... That's cute. I promise not to get violent with anyone else unless it's warranted."

The server led them to a room that appeared to be for banquets or special events. Legend pulled her chair out for her, then he took his seat.

"Okay, now, back to business. You were saying you want me to decorate an entire house," Diamond said.

# 5

Diamond was nervous, trying to keep her nerves and body under control. Before Jakari came over causing all the ruckus, she was having a hard time not thinking about how sexy and domineering Legend was. Now that she's seen him angry and defending her honor, her body was in overdrive. She tried to get him to refocus on the point of them meeting so they could discuss it and she could be out of his space. The way he kept looking at her made her think that Legend knew that she was having illicit thoughts about him.

"I'm buying my sister a house. You're her favorite interior designer. I want—well, I need you."

"Why not let her decorate her own house? I'm sure she has her own ideas of what she wants her house to look like when she gets one."

"She doesn't have a decorating bone in her body. She's smart as fuck with the computers and shit like that. However, there are two things she doesn't know how to do, and that's walk in stilettos and decorate any-damn-thing. She stays showing me shit on your page. Believe me when I tell you she'll be so excited if you decorate her house. Hell, she might be more excited about you decorating it than me giving it to her."

"I doubt that. She will be ecstatic about you giving her a house. I know I would."

"How much is it going to cost for you to do the house? When can you start?"

"I'll have to see the house first to know what I'm up against."

"I have to go out of town in two days. I know this is short notice, but will you be able to meet me tomorrow around two in the afternoon?" Legend asked.

Diamond took out her phone to check her schedule. She knew that she didn't have anything to do, but she didn't want to seem too anxious about meeting with him tomorrow.

"Two is good for me. I need to get your number so you can message me the address. When we get there, can you let me know what her favorite colors are? Does she like more modern or traditional type of pieces? I also need to know the date that everything needs to be done. Once I know all of that, I will discuss the price for my services."

"Sounds good to me."

Legend took his phone out and texted Diamond's phone. Diamond looked at him, wondering how the hell he got her number.

"I have my ways of getting the information that I want or need."

"If you had my number, why didn't you call me instead of waiting for me to reply to the message on Instagram?" Diamond asked.

"I just got your number last night. I also didn't want to intrude on your time. You had one more day not to respond to my message, and I was coming to knock on your door."

"Are you always this pushy?"

"No. I usually don't give a fuck if chicks respond to my messages or not. However, this is different. When it comes to putting a smile on my sister's face, I will walk through the pits of hell just to see it. She means everything to me, and the fact that she's staying focused and not being into all these nothing ass niggas out here makes me want to give her the world."

"That's sweet of you," she said.

The servers came with the food, placing the plates on the table. Diamond reached out for Legend's hands so she could say grace. Legend wasn't expecting her to do that. He prayed over his own food usually. However, this was the first time a woman had prayed over their food for him. He listened to Diamond say grace and was pleasantly surprised that she also asked that the Lord guide her heart and hands while she decorates the house. Once she said amen, they began to eat. He couldn't just let the night go by without him finding out the exact reason it took her so long to respond to his message.

"Can I ask you something?" he asked.

"You just did ask me something, but yeah, you can ask me another question."

"What was it that had your attention to the point that you didn't reply to my message?"

"It's really bothering you that I didn't respond to you as quick as you wanted me to, isn't it?"

"Hell yeah it is. I have never had to wait this long for anyone to respond to me. Then, on top of the fact that I'm trying to spend money, a lot of money with your company, I would think you would respond in twenty-four to forty-eight hours."

"To be totally truthful, I was packing up the guy that had approached our table things that were at my house. I'm the reason for his limp."

"You hit him with a bat in the leg or something?"

"No. It was more like a bullet to the knee," she said.

"Damn. What the fuck did he do?"

"Now you're just being nosy. I was fed up with him and all his shit. Women, especially black women, can take a lot on and still carry the load with grace. However, we get to the point when all the unnecessary shit has to go. I was making those adjustments while you were counting how many hours it took for me to respond to your message. Did I kill your ego, even though I didn't mean to? If I did, I'm sure you have someone or a few someones to help you feel better."

"You almost hurt my ego, but here we are, and my ego is intact. How's your food?"

"It's good. I didn't expect for a seafood salad to be packed with so much meat. I'm full, but I can't stop wanting to taste another bite."

"Don't force yourself to eat it all. You can take some of it home if you want."

"How did you know I liked seafood?" Diamond asked.

"You already forgot that my sister is a stalker when it comes to you. She talks about you so much that I think you're her shero or some shit."

"That's laying it on a little thick." Diamond laughed.

"You'll understand and see it when you meet her. She's gonna be flipping out like she's meeting Oprah or some-damn-body famous."

"Don't be jealous. I'm sure she admires you way more than she does me."

Legend only nodded in agreement, but he knew she was wrong in her assumption. She would see it soon enough, and he would happily tell her "I told you so" when the time came. The rest of the evening, Legend and Diamond stayed in the isolated room talking and laughing as if they were old friends catching up. She momentarily forgot about her issues, and he did the same with his. When it was time for them to part ways, neither wanted the night to end. Legend had surprisingly found the one woman in the world that didn't care that he was Legend or about the amount of money that the rumors around town said he had. She was a rare female and a live walking and talking diamond in the rough. He walked her to her car, told her to text him when she got home safe, and watched her pull of before walking to his. Laughter came over him when his phone started ringing. It could only be Alannah or Justin calling to see how the meeting had gone.

"Hello," Legend answered.

"Nigga, how much decorating do you have her doing?"

"What are you talking about?"

"I'm just asking. You said the meeting was at least two hours ago, and your black ass hasn't pulled up yet, which is why I asked that. Now answer the fucking question," Justin said, laughing.

"Man, I initially wanted her to decorate Alannah's house, but on the plane to Cali, I think I need to make a list of shit to buy just for her to decorate."

"Here your ass go. It isn't like you can do anything with her on that level. We all know London is the one walking around here claiming you. Shorty doesn't seem like the type to take a back seat to a delusional girlfriend," Justin said.

"I don't have a fucking girlfriend," Legend replied as he closed the car door and put on his seat belt.

"Pay attention while I'm talking, man. I said the word delusional. I know you heard me."

"Just like I know you heard me. Why are you sitting outside of my house?"

"I found out some more details on that Cali meeting. We have to go over it before the sun comes up. This shit is going to blow your mind. I read through it, and I still can't believe it."

"Is it that fucked up?"

"Hell yeah. It's so much shit that there's no fucking light at the end of the tunnel."

"Come on, Justin. Why you gotta fuck up my night? I just locked down the one designer that my sister loves and here your black ass come," Legend fussed.

Legend was on top of the world until he answered the phone. Now that Justin had said that, he wished he would've let it go to voicemail. He knew that he was going to have to face whatever it was that Justin wanted to tell him, but he would love to be ignorant to whatever was in that folder until he got home.

"Stop crying like a little ass girl. You know how this shit goes. You gotta stay two steps ahead. Now get your black ass over here so I can still go home and fuck somebody's daughter tonight."

Justin ended the call before Legend could say anything smart back to him. He wasn't in a rush to get home, but he damn sure wanted to get to the bottom of what the hell Carlito had going on.

# 6

"Are you going to tell me what the hell is going, on or do you want me to read all this shit instead of taking my black ass to bed?" Legend asked Justin as they took their seats.

"I know I told you that Carlito was talking to the feds and making it seem like you're the kingpin instead of him. I just found out tonight that there's more."

"The nigga is making it seem like it's me to protect his own ass. What else could there be?" Legend asked.

"I'm glad you asked that. He's making it seem like you're skimming money off the top to the other cartels. Not only is he wanting you to take the fall, but he's also covering his tracks, making sure no one will believe you when you try to tell them the truth or want to work with you because, in their eyes, you're a thief."

"You got to be fucking joking. Why the fuck can't I blow this nigga's head off, man? I need to just cut his ass off and not fucking take any calls or go to that stupid ass meeting."

"Nah. If you do that, then he'll know something's up and get spooked."

"I don't want to be around his snake ass period. Carlito is the last person I would think could be a snitch or even talking to the fucking feds. You know all the shit he taught us. Now he's flawed as fuck. This is making me rethink everything. I hate this shit. In this game, anyone can turn on you. That's the first thing he said to us. Do you remember that shit? We were young as fuck back then."

"Do you think he knew he was talking about himself when he said that? I'm just saying, even if we didn't see him as a nigga that'll snitch back then, he knew he had limits. This shit is fucked any way you try to explain it. That nigga is the one that took us under his wing and shit. When everything comes out, even though we aren't with what he's doing, we're gonna be looked at as being right along with him. We need to give everybody else a heads-up, but we need to do it without Carlito knowing about it."

"That's the same shit that I was thinking. Does your contact know how far they are in the investigation? I need to know how much time I'm working with. There has to be a meeting, and it has to be soon. The longer we sit on this, the worse we're going to look," Legend said.

"So how are we gonna do this? You know Carlito has someone here watching how we move just to help him sleep better. There's no way we can pull off a meeting if they're watching."

Legend sat there thinking for a moment. There had to be a way out of this. If Carlito is talking to the feds, he knows that he'll never be able to show his face again in the same circle. He has to have a plan for what he'll do and where he'll go after everything comes out. If he has a plan, he'll need the help of someone he thinks he can trust to help him execute it. There was only one person—well, maybe two people that Carlito trusted to that level. Legend looked at Justin. They both looked at each other until Justin understood what wasn't being said.

"Fuck nah, man. I'm not going down that fucking road again, literally," Justin said as he shook his head.

"You know she'll tell your black ass anything if you give her some play. You're gonna have to take one for the team. That's the only way I see us coming out of this shit on top."

"You would see it as the only way. It's not your dick that's being compromised."

Justin kissed his teeth and shook his head. Just the thought of Celeste made him want to throw up. A few years after Carlito started mentoring Legend and Justin, he introduced them to his niece Celeste. She was a few years younger than Justin and immediately took a liking to him over Legend. She always said that Legend was the devil because of how mean he was when she was around. Justin was the one that she tried to be around whenever Carlito allowed her to be around. The more time that Legend and Justin spent at Carlito's California estate, the closer he and Celeste became. He was thinking that they were just hanging out while she was thinking they were building a bond with one another, a girlfriend-boyfriend type of bond.

One night, after one of Carlito's lavish parties, Justin ended up taking Celeste's virginity. That was the beginning of the end for them. They continued to have a sexual relationship for six months after that. Justin thought that Celeste understood that they weren't together when they weren't together. However, Celeste was in love with Justin. She starting using her uncle's jet to come see him with little or no notice at all. The last time she came to see him, he was on a date with a female. Celeste approached them, causing a scene that ended with the young lady that Justin was with having to go to the hospital to get thirteen stitches to close up the cheek that Celeste had sliced open. That was the last night that Justin saw her. However, she randomly sends him text messages as if they are just old friends, catching up from time to time. He swore that he would never take it there with her again. Now it seems that he spoke too soon.

"What are you going to do?" Legend asked.

"You know if I fuck her again, she may kill my ass this time.

Are you willing to sacrifice my life just to get her uncle at his own game?" Justin asked.

"This isn't about just beating Carlito. It's about our freedom. If you don't do this, I can guarantee that we'll be locked up when the chips fall."

"That crazy chick will cut my dick off this time. She's all possessive and shit when the dick is involved."

"Would you rather be dickless and locked up or dickless and free? At least if you're free, you can get one of those dick transplants. Don't be side-eyeing me. I saw a commercial on TV."

"Yeah, that's what you tell me. It's my dick in jeopardy, not yours. I'll do it, but if the crazy broad kills me, you have to kill her and her dumb ass uncle."

"I can do that. Now, can you get out of my house so I can take my ass to bed? I have to meet Diamond at Alannah's house tomorrow."

"Oh shit. You need your beauty rest with your 'I need a love connection' ass. You don't need to be starting no love shit until we get this shit under wraps. I'm not trying to tell you what to do, but there's no need to get her all in love with you just for the cartels to come fuck shit up. Once we get this shit straight, then I'll be your best man as you cry while she walks down the aisle. I'm gonna bounce. Call me tomorrow after you're little design date, soft ass nigga," Justin joked before leaving the office.

Legend sat at his desk, thinking about what Justin just said. He knew Justin was right about this. Getting to know Diamond beyond her being the interior designer that Alannah loves was going to have to wait. There were more pressing issues for Legend to handle. Once everything was settled though, he was coming for Ms. Diamond full force.

Diamond googled the address that Legend sent her. It was in a part of town that she had planned on visiting, but she hadn't yet.

The average value of a house in this area, which some would consider a mini mansion, was around one point three million dollars. When she saw that, she knew that she had to change her mind from coming in the sweatsuit that she had planned to meet Legend in. She chose to put on something cute but comfortable. She chose to put on an above-the-knee bodycon gray dress with a pair of white and gray shell-toed Adidas shoes. She was sure to pick up her notebook on the way out. During the ride, she chose to ignore the phone calls from Ashera. She didn't need her nasty words invading her thoughts while she tried to work. Ashera and all her questions would have to wait until after the walk-through.

It took Diamond twenty minutes to make it to the house. She saw Legend standing on the porch doing something on his phone. Today, she got a chance to see what he was driving. Last night, she had already pulled off when he got to his car. She walked up to the porch, checking out the Mercedes. When she got to the porch, Legend looked up after smelling the fragrance of lavender and vanilla in the air. When he looked up to see Diamond in her casual dress and sneakers, he got sidetracked. All her curves were on display for anyone with eyes. That fact didn't sit too well with Legend. He wasn't expecting for her to come looking casually sexy. Now that she was standing in front of him, he wanted her to go home and change, but he knew requesting that would be a reach.

"Do you always come to walk-throughs dressed like that?" he asked, skipping the pleasantries and small talk.

"Good afternoon, Mr. Legend. The way I'm dressed has nothing to do with the task at hand. I wanted to be comfortable, so this was my choice. What's the matter with what I have on?" Diamond asked as she let her free hand caress the side of her body.

When she put the dress on, Legend checking her out never crossed her mind. The way he was looking at her sent chills all over her body. She stood there waiting for him to answer her question because she wanted to know what his problem was. It wasn't that his opinion mattered to her, but she wondered if he was as hot and bothered as she was. She smiled as the anticipation of his words grew. Legend looked her in the eye, licked his lips, bit his bottom lip, and winked at her.

"It's all good. If you like it, I love it. I'm just wondering if you go out like this often. Usually, chicks wear a jacket or something with what you have on."

"I wanted to be comfortable, like I said before. Are we going to stand here talking about my clothing choice, or are we going in to get this house decorated?" Diamond asked.

Legend chuckled at her retort. He wanted to grab her by the throat, tongue her down, and tell her to put some respect on his fucking name. However, now is not the time to let his dick control his actions. Also, he had agreed to clearing up this Carlito issue before he pushed up on Diamond. He opened the door, stepping to the side, allowing her to walk in the house before him. As she walked by, he was enjoying the view of her ass.

# 7

Justin was busy trying to get more information on Carlito's deal with the alphabet boys. Justin had three distant family members that worked for both the DEA and the FBI. They all knew what Justin was into, which is the main reason they always wanted to "help" him when they could. Justin and Legend learned a long time ago that being loud, flashy, and always wanting to be seen will get you knocked off or locked up quick as hell. While Legend had a thing for Jordans and cars, Justin had a thing for black art. His house was decorated with various portraits of black kings and queens, along with paintings that were created by black artists. Justin found peace in the paintings and art on his walls. However, today, he couldn't look to his walls to find any type of emotion other than anger.

Carlito was a father figure to Justin. Hearing and reading this information about his deal hurt Justin more than he had been hurt before. Coming up in the game, Justin thought he had two people he could rely on. Now that reality was setting in, he only had one person he could count on, and that's Legend. Legend has been standing with Justin since they were nine years old. Nothing along the way has broken that friendship. He knew that Carlito's actions have hurt Legend worse than it did him. Now was Justin's chance to rectify a wrong that wasn't his. He would do it, even if it meant connecting with a woman that he promised that he would stay away from. Picking up the phone, he dialed the numbers that he knew would surely start his days of endless drinking and nights of questioning the decisions he's made in life.

"Well, this is a surprise. Hello, Justin. Are you ready to talk to me about why you pushed me to act out when I last saw you?" Celeste asked.

"Celeste, I've been thinking about that night a lot lately. I see where I was wrong in all of that. Now, after all the shit that's been going on in the world, with the cops killing us, those white folks storming the capital and getting away with it, and this global warming shit, all of that made me decide to bury the hatchet with everyone that's pissed off with me. You're the first on that list."

Justin was grabbing at straws with reasons he would be reaching out to her. He hoped she was gullible enough welcome him back in her world with open arms.

"Who was she to you, Justin?"

Justin rolled his eyes because he wasn't planning on talking about the chick he was with that night. Truthfully, she wasn't anyone special. Justin couldn't even say that they were just friends, because they were barely that. Maybe the relationship could've grown into something, but Celeste cutting her face put an end to that. The next day, Justin went to the hospital to talk to her, but she cursed him out and told him to forget that he ever knew her. That's exactly what he did.

"She was just a friend. You shouldn't have cut her without knowing what was going on. You have a short fuse, even when it's not needed. That shit was fucked up, and you know it was," Justin told her.

"I did feel bad when my uncle called me fussing at me for what I did, but at the time, it made sense for me to do it. If I could turn back time, I would wait and let both of you explain before cutting her face up."

Justin shook his head at how casually she said that. How can a person be so casual about permanently disfiguring someone's face? *If this bitch kills me, I'm gonna haunt the fuck out of Legend's ass.*

"We don't have to keep talking about that. I know you've reached out to me from time to time, but I wasn't ready to communicate with you again. Now, I'm sure I can be the man that you need me to be. Let me prove it to you that we can be happily ever after," Justin said, nearly choking on his words.

"Just when I had made peace with the fact that we'll never see each other again, here you come calling me wanting our old thing back like in the movies," she said with a giggle that made Justin roll his eyes.

"Are you in Cali?" he asked.

"No, I'm not going back there until next week."

"Damn, I fly out to go there tomorrow. I was hoping that we could spend some time together. I guess we'll have to keep talking over the phone until we can see each other again."

"You're still going to go even though I'm not gonna be there?" Celeste asked.

"Come on, Celeste. You know that I have business to handle with your uncle. I was going before I made this call, so I'm goin' after. You know that nothing stops my money flow. That nothing includes you."

Celeste thought about what Justin was saying. She came to the conclusion that he was right. Even when they weren't making as much money as they are now, Justin never let anything come before business. That was one thing she never liked about Justin. In her mind, she was way too fine and freaky to play the number-two spot. She would nag him back then, but he never budged. Justin was never one to spare anyone's feelings, so it was totally up to her to continue to deal with him after his stance was made known to her. Just like all those years ago, she chose to stick by him. She wasn't giving up on him now. Actually, her plan was to lock him down, even if that meant acting like she was pregnant. She didn't want to do it, but if at any time she felt like he was getting away from her again, she would do it with her head held high.

"I guess some things never change. I thought that maybe you would've changed, even a little bit," she said, sighing loudly as if that was going to change Justin's mind.

"Ain't shit changing about me but the number on my bank account slips. If you can't be number-two quietly, then we can end this phone call now. I'll see you when I see you."

Justin was hoping that she would take him up on his offer and end the call. If she did, then he could tell Legend that she wasn't for it, and it would be the truth. However, he knew that would be too much like right if she did.

"Justin, you know I've always loved you. I'm in this with you all the way. I'll just have to come see you when you say it's cool for me to do so. You know I like to have all your time when I come out there, so tell Legend he's gonna have to find something to do when I get out there," Celeste said.

"Oh, I'll let him know for sure," Justin said as he shook his head. "Aye, let me get back with you later on. I have some stuff to handle before we get on the plane."

"Okay, make sure you call me back, Justin."

"I got you, Celeste."

Celeste was so happy that she didn't pay it any mind that Justin had ended the call before she could say her goodbyes in return. Justin, on the other hand, was dialing Legend's number to let him know that he owed him big time.

"Yeah, Justin," Legend answered.

"Nah, you need to put some respect on my damn name. I just talked to the looney ass broad. She's all for us getting back together. She's not going to be in Cali when we get out there. Well, that's what she said anyway."

"Why you say it like that? You don't believe her or something?" Legend asked.

"Hell nah I don't. She may not be there now, but I'll bet you two fresh hundred-dollar bills that her ass will be there by the time we get there. I told her that we would try to make shit work this time, so she's not trying to let too many days go by without being all up in my space."

Legend laughed at how stressed Justin sounded. He remembered how relieved he was when Carlito told him that he understood why he didn't want to continue seeing his niece after she cut that female's face. Now here he was, jumping back into the lion's den with his eyes wide open.

"You just called her, and we have to leave the day after tomorrow, right? Do you think she'll move that fast?" Legend asked.

"Nigga, I guarantee you she's packing right now. Her ass probably called Carlito for the jet to come get her from wherever her ass is now."

Legend continued to laugh at his friend's pain. Eventually, Justin got pissed listening to Legend's laughter, and he ended the call on him just like he had done Celeste. Legend laughed louder when he realized that Justin wasn't on the phone anymore. Alannah walked in the living room, wondering what the hell was so funny that made Legend laugh so hard. She wanted to ask but decided not to.

"Excuse me, Sir Laugh A Lot, I officially only have one more month before I find out what number I'll be in my graduating class. I know I'm in the top twenty. I just want to know where."

"I would've never thought that my lil' sister would grow up to be a fucking nerd. I was just happy to graduate from high school. I didn't give a fuck what number I was. I got my piece of paper and was out."

Alannah shook her head at her brother. It was crazy to her how much Legend was feared by people who didn't know how goofy he really was. She was intrigued by her brother. The fact that she knew him better than anyone else is what made her want to laugh when she heard outsiders speak on him. Alannah scrolled her Instagram timeline, wondering what kind of designs Diamond was going to post. She hadn't posted anything new in three days. Alannah was starting to have withdrawals. Legend noticed the irritated look on his sister's face.

"What's the matter with you?" he asked her.

"Diamond hasn't posted anything new in the last few days. I hope she's okay," Alannah said, sounding worried.

"You're turning into a fucking stalker, sis. That shit ain't cool. We don't stalk a motherfucking thing. Tighten up," Legend told her.

"I'm not stalking anyone. You act like I'm in love with her or something. I just love the fact that she's a black woman making her own lane in the world of interior design. No matter what everyone else is doing in the industry, she continues to do what she likes and how she likes to do it. Think about it, even in the fashion world, you have black designers that start out doing what they are inspired to do with their clothes. Eventually, that changes. They get on, and you start to see a shift in their work. It starts turning into what's selling or being more commercial. Diamond doesn't do that. Every time she posts something new, you can see her personality shine through. Even though you can tell that it's her work, all of her work is different as well."

Legend stood there looking at his sister. For the first time, he noticed how her face and eyes lit up while she was talking about Diamond's work. She never got excited about cyber security like that.

"Do you want to do interior design?" he asked her.

"What are you talking about?"

"You never look happy about that cyber shit that you went to school for. I would hate to see you working at a job you don't love because of what everyone else thinks."

"No, it's not like that. I love doing cyber security, but interior design is a potential hobby of mine. I could see myself doing it on the side here and there though, not full time though."

Legend nodded his head in understanding. There had to be

some signs that he had missed before now. If he had known, he would've tried to set something up so she could be an assistant to a designer or something. He wanted Alannah to have all the opportunities and advantages that he didn't have. Being a drug dealer was not on his list of probable occupations. This is the result of the cards that he was dealt. Although he did pretty good with what he had, it would be better if he wasn't on the wrong side of the law. The last thing Legend wanted to do was go down the road of what-ifs and what could've been. Right now, he was on the wrong side of the law, and that could possibly cause more problems with Carlito being on his bullshit.

# 8

Legend was on his way to the airport, and all he could think about was Diamond and Alannah. He knew that they would hit it off if they ever met. Since he was the link between the two, it was up to him to put things in motion. He had some time since he liked to get to the airport extra early. He made a turn and headed to Alannah's house that Diamond was working on. Even though he had a semi-legit reason to see her, he wanted to just see her period.

When he pulled up, he could hear music blasting as he walked to the front door. After he walked in, he looked at the three guys that were painting, giving them a head nod as he walked up the steps where the music was coming from. He found Diamond in the main bedroom. She was dressed in a baseball cap, a halter top, a pair of short shorts, and some Nike sneakers on her feet.

"I know them niggas downstairs didn't see you dressed like this," he said before he could stop himself.

Diamond was so wrapped in what she was doing that she didn't know he was in the room until he started talking.

"What are you doing here? I didn't expect you to come by on the first day of work. Is everything okay?" Diamond asked.

"I just came by because I was talking to my sister yesterday, and I think she could be a good assistant for you. She's getting her degree and has a job lined up, but I think her passion is in interior design. Once she sees the house and all that, is there any way she can come on as assistant for small projects or whatever?"

"If she wants to, I don't have a problem with that. You could've called me to say that. You didn't have to come all the way over here."

Diamond was confused as to why Legend made the trip all the way over here just to tell her that. He was dressed casually, so maybe he was out running errands or something like that. Diamond could see a slight outline of his penis under his pants. Her mind wondered if he was hard because of her or was he not hard at all. If he wasn't, she was definitely going to have to stay away from him. Legend was walking around with a true *legend* in his pants.

"You know that shit is rude, right?" he asked her as he readjusted himself and licked his lips when her eyes finally moved up to meet his.

"Wh—Huh? What are you talking about?" she stuttered as the room began to get hot.

"I'm talking about how your eyes were just focused on my dick. I could pull it out for you and kill all that curiosity I saw in your eyes. Better yet, you could ask to see it using that sexy voice you chicks be using all the damn time," Legend said as he smiled at how uncomfortable Diamond was right now.

"You are a man that doesn't lack self-confidence. That's for sure. Is there anything else you need to tell me? I need to get back to work," Diamond said.

Legend laughed at how she deflected everything that he just said. He would let her have it for now. Once all his ducks were in a row, her time was up. It didn't matter to Legend if she was ready or not.

"I'm about to go out of town for a few days. You can text me updates or your dreams whenever you feel like it. I'll be by here after I get settled to see you and the progress."

Diamond rolled her eyes at him saying the word progress. It was becoming apparent to her that Legend liked to fuck with her. If he wanted to fuck with her, then she was going to do the same to him.

"Just make sure you're ready and waiting," she moaned.

Legend stopped in his tracks. He knew what she was trying to do, but she's not the one that was running this show. It was time that she understood that there were boundaries between them, even if their relationship wasn't fully established. Diamond was going to learn that Legend had her mind so gone to the point that he could make her body do things that she never thought of. However, today she was gonna learn not to fuck with Legend unless she was ready to FUCK Legend.

Diamond thought she had gotten away with it. She had turned around and started doing what she was doing before Legend came in the room. When she realized she had fucked up, her chest was pressed against the wall, and his hard, long, thick dick was pressed against her ass. Diamond's body came alive as the feeling of his breath and beard against her neck became more consistent. Legend kissed her shoulder, then her neck, as Diamond's heart began to race. The unexpected sound of Legend growling in her ear both turned her on and gave her pause.

"If I was the type of nigga they say I am, I would say fuck that damn flight and teach you some manners. Never tease a nigga that wants to beat that pussy up, Diamond. It always starts off as playing and ends with you being knocked up, getting ya back blown out in the bathroom at the baby shower. Go play with somebody that ain't trying to wife your thick ass," Legend whispered before sucking on her entire ear.

Once he heard her moan for real, he eased off her and left her in the room alone. Diamond had to stop her head from spinning and try to get her body under control. The nipples were hard, her panties were soaked, and her mind was stuck on how much meat was just pressed against her. Fanning herself and taking a few deep breaths wasn't working. Diamond went downstairs to get a bottle of water out of the refrigerator. Her mind was so focused on needing water that she didn't see the amused looks that the painters were giving her. She opened the bottle and drank more than half of it immediately. When she was done, they were looking at her like she was crazy.

"What?" she asked.

"Nothing, D. You just look a little thirsty after homie left. What the hell was going on up there?" one of the guys said, followed by laughter from them all. Diamond had never been so embarrassed in her life. There was nothing that she could say to refute what was implied. She was not ready for them to say anything to her. Granted, they were Ashera's cousins, but they never really said much to her that wasn't work related. Diamond always wondered about how quiet they were around her.

"I could always find another team to paint my projects."

That response only made them laugh harder.

Legend and Justin got settled in their first-class seats. Justin was throwing Legend a serious side-eye, which he was ignoring. The flight attendant came by to make sure they didn't need anything, and sure enough, when she was far enough not to hear, Justin started his questions.

"Where the hell were you?" Justin asked.

"You're straight sounding like London right now. I was handling some business. You know we don't trade details. so don't ask."

"Were you with Diamond?"

"Nigga, what is up with all the questions? I'm here and my black ass is on the plane. Stop acting like a female."

"You got me out here about to go see this crazy ass broad,

and you act like you didn't want to show up. I thought I was getting set up to go out here on my own with your late ass."

"I had to go make sure shorty was straight being that she just started working on Alannah's house. Traffic held me up. That's all. Are you done questioning me? You need to be worried about not throwing up when Celeste wants to seal y'all's rekindling."

"Low blow. That's a real low blow. I noticed you called Diamond shorty, but I also noticed how you keep side-eying me when I say her name. It looks like I'll be the one that'll make the speech at y'all's wedding. She's getting under your skin. I wonder how that shit is gonna work if we don't beat Carlito at his own game. Getting away from Celeste once and for all is my motivation to get this shit wrapped up as soon as possible. Let Diamond be yours," Justin said.

After ordering two drinks and laying back to get some shut-eye during the flight, Legend was happy that Justin took that as permission for him to shut the fuck up. Celeste had sent Justin a text message saying that she had a surprise for him, which let him know that she would be there all happy and shit when they got to Carlito's estate. He had to take about six drinks to Legend's two in order to relax. He still didn't sleep for the rest of the flight, but he wasn't as nervous about landing in California. Justin never said anything to Legend about it, but seeing Celeste slice someone's face open in the name of love scarred him mentally. Before that night, he wasn't fond of love, and he went out of his way to avoid it at any cost. In his mind, love caused you to act irrational, unhinged, and all the other words that meant crazy as fuck. Celeste was the reason he never let anyone get too close and was known for the fuck and duck. She was the epitome of the devil, and now he had to play nice with her. Legend didn't understand just how much he was asking of his friend. The flight attendant announced the impending landing with the current time and weather in Las Angeles, California. Justin shifted in his seat, trying to remain calm on the outside, although he was anything but.

"I want you to know I appreciate you putting yourself in harm's way like this. I know she doesn't like my black ass, or else I would try to finesse her crazy ass. Just know that while you're doing that, I'll be playing nice with Carlito's ass."

Every time Legend thought about Carlito giving him up to the feds instead of himself, it burned Legend up. There was a thin line between love and hate for sure. Carlito was oblivious to the fact that sides had been chosen.

# 9

Carlito was sitting in his grand room, waiting for Legend and Justin to arrive. When he first agreed to doing this, he never thought that his emotions and nerves would have him sick to his stomach. When he signed on the dotted line, he never thought things would get this far. Basically, he never thought he would live beyond six months after signing the affidavit. His mother always told him to never listen to the doctors because they never had the last say. He laughed at the fact that, even from beyond the grave, his mother was showing him that he should've paid more attention to what she said. Looking up at the clock, he noticed that it was time for the fellas to arrive. He drank the last of the brown liquor from his glass before heading to the front door. It was showtime. He had to get through this meeting and the weekend without letting on that he was working with the feds or that he was dying.

Before opening the front door, he cleared his throat and said a prayer. He was very aware of the consequences of his actions. Even though he was a father figure to both men, there was no doubt in his mind that they would kill him and grieve at his funeral. They were everything that he had groomed them to be.

As Carlito turned the knob and stepped out onto the porch,

he was grateful for the little time he had left to be alive. The California sun was being an unruly bitch today. Carlito welcomed the warmth against his skin. On most days, the side effects of the chemotherapy wouldn't allow him to stand out here beyond ten minutes. However, the medicated sunblock that he put on was helping him withstand the heat. Carlito stood firm as the cars pulled up. He understood that Legend and Justin were going to have their eyes on him. He couldn't let on that he was in any kind of pain, or there would be questions for sure. Legend stepped out of the back seat of the Cadillac STS with the confidence and aura that he always had. When he looked at Carlito standing on the porch, he smiled, quickening his steps to meet Carlito with an embrace. Carlito closed his eyes, letting his emotions of this possibly being the last embrace overcome him briefly. A similar embrace followed with Justin before they all walked into the house.

"How was the flight? I could never keep taking commercial flights like you two do. I'm too old for all that shit."

Legend and Justin shared a look as they followed Carlito into the house. They both got the feeling that something was off about Carlito. There was a heavy aura in the room. Neither of them voiced their concerns. They were going to let everything play out. Time always revealed everything. They just had to have patience.

"Long, boring, and small ass cups of more soda than liquor as always. We come out here enough. You would think we know a few of the flight attendants on a more-intimate level, but no such luck. It's a damn shame I have all these frequent flyer miles, and I still haven't gotten my card punched for the air fucking club," Justin said with a laugh.

"That's the mile high club. If you would take up my offer for me to send the jet, you could be a member of it by now. I know I am," Carlito said with a smile.

"Too much information, old man," Legend interjected.

"Come to my office with me. We can get business out of the

way before you two go find a club to hang out at tonight. This shouldn't be long. I told you that you could've flown out here for a day instead of three."

"That flight is too damn long for us to do a short turnaround like that. Let me find out you're trying to get rid of us," Justin joked.

"I would never want to get rid of you two. You're the closet things to sons that I have. Whatever I do, I do it in the name of love that I can promise you both," Carlito said seriously.

"Is everything okay? I know we came here to talk about business, but something's off. Are you going to tell us what's going on with you?" Legend questioned.

"Y'all are here for the next few days. We have time to talk about other stuff, but right now, let's talk business. I wanted you two here so I could tell you face-to-face that I'm preparing for my exit. I would like for you both to step in and take over for me. I'm fully aware that this is not what you want to do until you're my age, which is why I asked you to come here so we could discuss it."

"When you say exit, I don't get the feeling that you're talking about retirement. What's up with that?" Justin asked.

"I'm an old man. We all have to die sooner or later. In my case, it happens to be sooner. That's a discussion for another time. It's more important that we discuss what options do I have."

"What do you mean?" Justin asked.

"I just told you both that I'm ready to hand the keys over to all that I control to you both. Neither one of you moved an inch or even asked for any details. It's safe to say that either you don't want the keys to what I have, you want to build your own, or you want out altogether. Which is it?"

"Legend's in love, so I'm sure he's going legit. I haven't decided either way yet. Love isn't in the cards for me yet. I also know that if I stay in this shit too long, the road ends in places I don't want to be. If I end up in jail, I would rather be there because of my shit and not because some corner boy doesn't want to do five years. I just need some time to think about it. You're not gonna get your answer on this trip, but like I said, I'll weigh my options."

"That's all I can ask," Carlito said before turning his attention to Legend. "Who is the woman that's stolen Legend's heart?"

"This dude is lying. I'm not in love. The one he's talking about is the woman that's decorating Alannah's house for me. His ass is just doing the most, as usual."

"Notice that he never said he didn't want her though." Justin laughed.

"Never put love on the back burner. You'll find yourself old and alone before you know it. Take it from me. If I could go back in time, there would be a lot of things that I would change. Walking away from the one woman that loved me would be the first thing I'd change."

"If she loved you, why walk away?" Legend asked.

"I loved the adrenaline rush that moving up the cartel ladder gave me more than I did her. She wanted me to walk away, and at the time I was young, dumb, and wanting to assert myself as a man. Instead of seeing her for what she was, I thought she was trying to change me. That is one of my many regrets. Taking you two under my wing and grooming you to be the men that you are is one of my proud moments. No matter what goes on and where we all end up, always remember that you two are my sons. I have you both as beneficiaries on my life insurance policies and detailed instructions in the will."

"Why are you talking like you're gonna die tonight? Can you be any more gloomier than right now?" Justin asked.

Carlito chuckled, then got up to make him a drink. There was more that he wanted to say, but now was not the time. He had already said too much. The questions were clear on their faces. However, neither of them questioned Carlito yet. Carlito knew that their minds were already working to try to come to some sort of good explanation on their own. He had just revealed too much, and now he was running out of time. The longer Legend and Justin stayed, the more questions he would have to answer. He had the answers, but he was not ready for what those answers led to. There were heavy consequences for Carlito's actions. It was a shame that death hadn't come to help him escape what he knew the future held. Having Legend and Justin look at him like the rat he had become was a consequence worse than death. Carlito never wanted to be put in a class with the likes of Frank Lucas, Alpo Martinez, or Sammy Gravano. Those men were pop culture celebrities for working with the police. They were still just rats to Carlito. Now, he was just a rat as well.

"Death waits for no one. That's why you must always be prepared."

Carlito noticed that Legend was quiet and looked like he had a lot on his mind. For a moment, Carlito wondered if Legend had any information of his impending deal with the police. Pushing that thought out of his mind, he continued to look at Legend. He had come so far from the little slick-talking hustler that Carlito had pulled off the corner because of how much dope he was pushing even when he was a corner boy.

"What's on your mind, Carlito?" Legend asked.

"I was just remembering when I pulled you two off the corner all those years ago. Petey was pissed because I took his most-profitable workers off the corner. There wasn't shit he could do besides be mad though. Shit, after that day, he knew his days running the block were numbered. Y'all took the man's blocks with him right there thinking that he had everything on lock," Carlito said with a chuckle.

"You know he still feels some type of way about that shit. It wasn't up to us. His bitch ass should've seen the shit coming," Legend said as he shook his head.

"True. Everybody seen it but him. Even a few of his jump offs pushed up on me talking about they knew we were the next up for running the block. If they knew, his ass had to know," Justin chimed in.

All of them laughed together. Carlito was remembering the meeting where the announcement was made that Petey was no longer the one running that particular block. It was wild how he put on a whole scene because he felt disrespected by "the youngins", which is what he called Legend and Justin. Legend shook his head as he recalled how everything went down.

"It was fucked up because had he put on a show like that a year later, we would've killed his ass on the spot. Instead, he got the soft Legend," Justin said as he laughed.

"I took his fucking kneecaps. How the hell is that soft. That motherfucker couldn't walk on his own for over a year. I know he still gets pissed when it rains." Legend laughed.

"Hey, guys." Celeste walked in the room all smiles and full of energy.

Carlito rolled his eyes because he knew it was about to be some bullshit between her and Justin. They weren't getting along as far as Carlito knew. Legend sighed as he tossed her a head nod, which prompted her to kiss her teeth. Justin sat slightly uncomfortable in the chair. Celeste plopped down on Justin's lap, causing Carlito to choke on his drink.

"I see I've missed some things. What is all of this?" Carlito asked.

"Uncle Carlito, Justin and I are back together. If I have my way, I'll be a married woman by next year."

Justin stood up, allowing Celeste to fall to the floor. Legend doubled over with laughter. Carlito was shocked as well as amused.

"See? This is that bullshit. Just because we're on sort of good terms, you can't be around here making plans like that. I never mentioned the word marriage, so you're either smoking some strong meth, or you're marrying somebody else. Let me know right now if you're gonna be on some bullshit so I can get the fuck on," Justin barked as he looked down at her.

"I can't believe you just embarrassed me like that," Celeste whined as she stood to her feet.

"You can't be embarrassed when you knew that bullshit wasn't gonna fly with me. Celeste, you know me well enough to know that I'm not holding my words in front of anyone. You come out your mouth with that bullshit, then look at me crazy for what exactly? I know you didn't think I would be like 'yeah' or some dumb shit like that. You got your own life fucked up for even trying that shit."

Justin was pissed. Here it was he thought that Celeste would act like she had one ounce of good sense. Evidently, she had shit for brains when it came to her and Justin. Who the fuck comes at a man about marriage after they have a few short phone conversations? Legend stopped laughing long enough to fix a drink. This shit was more amusing than watching one of those ghetto ass videos online.

"What changed, Justin? I remember you calling me, trying to talk yourself out of snapping my niece's neck for what she did. We agreed then that you two are like oil and water; y'all don't mix. However, she's under the impression that you and her are going to be doing more than mixing. Can you fill me in?" Carlito questioned.

"It's a long story," Justin mumbled.

"How does that song go? The song that everyone is listening to now..." Carlito snapped his fingers as he tried to remember the song. He looked at the watch on his wrist with a smile on his face. "I just looked at my watch, I've got time to day," he continued.

Legend was back on the floor laughing. Carlito had to laugh as well. He knew that Justin and Legend found it funny that he was up to date on the new music. Justin shook his head as he got up to find a bottle of liquor. More than a drink or two was needed right now.

# 10

Diamond was opening her front door when she heard steps behind her. Shaking her head, she slipped her keys back into her purse, then took out her gun before turning around. When she saw Jakari standing in front of her, she rolled her eyes.

"How about asking me how I'm doing since you shot me and left me to die the other day?"

"I saw you a day or two ago, I know you're not dead. You're getting around, so you're obviously doing just fine. Why are you here, Jakari?"

"I'm here to find out when you're gonna let me come back home. I know I fucked up. I apologized. What more do you want from me?"

"I want you to leave me the fuck alone. Can you do that to the best of your ability, please?"

Jakari wasn't giving up on what he and Diamond had. She was the best thing that had happened to him. He should've taken his ass home. Now he was paying for it. Jakari knew that he could never be completely faithful to Diamond, but he didn't have to flaunt his bullshit in her face like he'd been doing. The one thing he never thought of was happening to him; Diamond was finally leaving his ass for good. All the other times, he would've been back in the house by now.

"I can't do that, so you're gonna have to name something else."

"There isn't shit else that I want from you. I just want to go on with my life without you in it. Simple."

"Look me in my eyes and tell me that you see the pain and loneliness that you're putting on me right now. We're good together. We're a team," Jakari lied.

"A team, huh? Are you sure about that?"

"Hell yeah. I had your back, and you had mine. Stop playing with me, Diamond."

Jakari didn't like the way Diamond was trying to play him right now. He was trying to make shit up to her, but she was paying him no mind.

"When is trash day?" she asked.

"Huh, what the fuck are you talking about?"

"You just said we were a team, right? If we were a team, you should know what day of the week you put the trash out. Oh, I have an easy one for you. How much is the cable and internet bill?"

Jakari rolled his eyes because he knew what she was doing. She was trying to ask him shit that she knew he didn't know to make him look bad.

"Diamond, come on," he groaned.

"Come on, what, Jakari? You don't know, because you've never paid one bill in here, you didn't put the trash out, or none of that other shit you should've been doing. It got to the point where you stopped asking me if I had all the mortgage money."

"You're always on that independent woman shit, so I let you do you. There isn't shit wrong with that. If I would've tried to pay a bill or two, you were gonna give me grief behind that. You're always listening to your dumb ass friend, even though I keep telling you she's jealous of you."

"We're not talking about her. This conversation is about you and this imaginary team that we were."

"Were? You said that like it's permanent."

"Oh, it is. You and I will never be together again. I would rather suck a dick infested with red ants," Diamond told him.

"Damn, that's fucked up. I do whatever you ask me to do just so I can get back with you. I promise I can treat you better this time around," Jakari lied.

"You need to tell me where you were that you couldn't come home or call. It was like you just said 'fuck Diamond'."

"No, it wasn't like that," he pleaded.

"Yes it was. You're still standing here, but you haven't told me where you were yet. Get out of my face before I shoot you again. I'm tired of motherfuckers like you playing with me. Doormat Diamond is gone. Move the fuck around."

"Oh, is that right. Why is she gone now? I bet it's because of that motherfucking Legend. He's done pumped your head all up. Now you're too good for a nigga like me. I see how you're changing all behind that nigga. Is that what type of female you are?"

Diamond laughed at Jakari so hard that tears were streaming down her face. She couldn't believe that he would stoop so low. Well, yes she could. Diamond had been nothing but good to Jakari, only for him to disregard her feelings to run the street like he was a single man. Now he's grasping at straws, trying to guilt her into taking him back. Jakari was about to get his feelings hurt because Diamond wasn't buying what he was selling.

"Yup," she said, making sure to make the popping sound at the end of the word. "I'm done being the backbone for a boy in a man's body. Legend and I have nothing going on, so stop bringing him up. I'm tired of being everything to a nigga that I obviously meant nothing to. There's no reason for you to be out all night when you don't have a job or a hustle. Yet your ass was gone for multiple fucking nights. Make that shit make sense to me. Now you want to come by to try to plead your case on deaf ears. There's nothing over here for you or I to rekindle. Whatever we had is dead and gone, finito, over, caput."

The ringing of Diamond's cell phone interrupted the conversation. Jakari was low-key happy about that because he wasn't trying to hear what she was saying right now.

"Hello?" Diamond answered.

"When I ask you this question, I need you to think before you answer," Legend said.

"Okay. What's the question?"

"Why the fuck is that nigga at your house? Why are you entertaining him in the first place? Niggas love to act like they care after they get caught. Whatever he said, I can guarantee that it's all lies."

"I don't care or know why he's here. I have nothing for him or any other man that wants to waste the amount of good woman that I am."

"You still aren't telling me shit. He needs to get from in front of your house. When I say that, I'm talking about right now. It's bad enough he has a couple more days to live because I had other shit to handle. To see that he's being reckless with the little bit of time he has left shows me that I should've killed his ass the other night like I started to."

"Is all that necessary? That was nothing but a misunderstanding," Diamond questioned.

"A misunderstanding, huh? I guess you're right because his ass still doesn't understand. He's not supposed to be anywhere around you. I specifically told him that shit. His hardheaded ass misunderstood that too, right, Diamond?"

"How are you talking about all of this like it's nothing? What if the phones are tapped? You're incriminating yourself right now."

"Don't you worry your sexy ass about all that. I need you to get that motherfucker away from your house. If you see him out in the street, act like you don't know him. It's obvious that he doesn't respect boundaries, so it's in your hands now."

"If I don't do what you say, are you going to kill me too?"

"Nah. I'm just gonna have you out of work for a week," Legend said.

"I never figured that you're a woman beater."

"I'm not one of those."

"Why would I be out of work for a week?"

"It's gonna be hard for you to walk, stand, sit, and maybe even breathe after I get done with you. You don't have to worry about that right now. All that will come when the time is right and we will too. Diamond, get him away from your door now, or we're gonna have a misunderstanding," Legend said calmly before ending the call.

Diamond looked around, wondering how the hell did Legend know Jakari was there in the first place. She didn't see a car or person out of place.

"Diamond, what the fuck is up with you? Did you forget I was standing here?"

"No, but you need to leave and not come back. We're over, Jakari. Leave me the fuck alone."

Diamond didn't wait for him to respond before she walked in the house, closing and locking the door behind her. She was almost to the table when her phone alerted her to a new text message.

***Him:*** *Following directions is sexy as fuck. Good girl.*

Diamond shook her head as she headed to her bedroom.

❧

Justin was in his room for the night, still pissed about Celeste and her bullshit. Legend and Carlito thought it was funny, but they didn't understand that Celeste was dead ass serious about marrying Justin.

"I'm gonna have to kill this bitch. Then I'll have to kill Carlito behind his crazy ass niece," Justin said to himself.

He was pacing the floor, trying to wrap his head around how

bad of an idea it was for him to contact Celeste. Justin understood that there was something wrong in her head. She was fixated on him and only him. Interacting with her was only going to make her act out more than she ever had. He had a gut feeling that shit was about to get all fucked up with Celeste. Legend walked in the room with a mug on his face.

"What the fuck you got a mug on your face for? If anyone should be looking like that, it should be me. I'm telling you now that you I'm gonna kill her ass. After I do that, you're gonna buy me a damn yacht that I can take out on the harbor. After this bullshit, I'll need a lot of days of relaxation. Next time, you're gonna take one for the team, motherfucker."

"Shit, you never know. She might be good for you in the long run," Legend joked.

Legend could joke all he wanted, but Justin wasn't in the mood for the bullshit.

"Yeah, okay. I want you to remember I told you this first. I'm gonna have to off the bitch. I hate using that word, but it's the truth. You don't believe me, even after I told you her ass was coming here. Bam! Here her ass is, talking about we're getting married. I've barely talked to the broad. Her dingy ass probably already has the dress picked out. I'm telling you, this shit is all bad. On top of that, you heard Carlito talking like he's gonna die. What the fuck was up with that?" Justin questioned.

"That's what I came in here to talk to you about. Hearing him talk about wills and shit threw me off. Why the hell is he talking like that if he's working for the feds? It sounds like he dying to me," Legend revealed.

He had been thinking that Carlito was holding back more information than just his situation with the law. Legend noticed everything about Carlito. He was looking a little thin and not looking them in the eye while he was talking. All of that, in addition to the uncomfortable atmosphere, let Legend know that things were off. From the looks of things, snitching was the last thing on Carlito's mind.

"Do you think that's why he called us out here? To tell us that he's dying?"

Legend shrugged his shoulders while Justin shook his head. The two men sat in the room, lost in their thoughts about what was really going on with Carlito. The only confirmation that they needed was the fact that their guts were telling them both that this meeting was only for Carlito to tell them goodbye. Legend was having an internal battle because he had his mind settled on killing Carlito for being a snitch, but seeing him and hearing Carlito talk about his will and insurance policy hit him different.

# ❧ 11 ❧

Jakari was driving around, blowing off steam, after walking away from Diamond's yard. He knew that had to be Legend on the phone for her to leave him outside like that. He heard Diamond both times when she said that she and Legend were only friends, but her actions told him they were definitely fucking. He couldn't believe Diamond was allowing Legend to run her like this. Legend may have been that nigga on the streets, but when it came to Diamond, Jakari felt that she was his and his alone. Not even Legend could come between them—well, that's what he was trying to tell himself. He pulled up to the corner store, parking in front, making sure to speak to the fellas hanging out in front.

"Aye, Jakari, how long have you and Diamond been broken up?" one of the guys asked.

"Nigga, who the fuck are you?"

"I'm Lonnie, Ashera's cousin. I know you remember me because I was the one that helped Diamond pack your shit one of those times y'all took a break or whatever."

The rest of the guys laughed at that comment. Jakari didn't think shit was funny at all.

"Fuck you. How the hell you know we broke up? Ashera had

to be the one to tell you that shit. She stays running her damn mouth about what Diamond and I have going on," Jakari complained.

"Nah. I do painting for Diamond whenever she needs it. This morning, we were painting this big ass house, and that nigga Legend came in like he owned the motherfucker. Come to think of it, he probably do, but anyway, he went upstairs where Diamond was for a little while. After he left, she came downstairs looking flustered as fuck. If he didn't fuck her, he damn sure did something to her thick ass."

"What the fuck are you talking about?"

"You heard what the fuck I said. I know y'all not rocking no more because if y'all were, she wouldn't have let that nigga get close to her."

"You're just assuming shit. If you didn't see them all over each other, you're just guessing about what happened."

Jakari was trying to come up with something to prove Lonnie wrong, but he couldn't come up with anything.

"That nigga Legend had shorty so shook that she had to go outside and get some air. I've known Diamond for a long time, and I've never seen her like that."

"Diamond and I will be back tight just like always. She's just trying to play hard right now."

"This nigga standing here trying to play like shit ain't over. If we see that shit is over, then you gotta see it too," another guy said.

Jakari felt like a fool in front of all these guys that he didn't know.

"Fuck y'all. Diamond and I have been rolling strong all this time. That doesn't change overnight."

"We'll see. You know Legend is that motherfucker out here. It looked like more was going on up those stairs, but you don't have to believe me," Lonnie said.

Jakari walked in the store, not wanting to entertain what Lonnie was saying anymore. Legend was gonna fuck around and have Jakari go find his ass. He walked to the back of the store where the cold beers were. The money he had was running low, so he chose to purchase two of the cheapest beers in the store. Jakari was so stressed that he opened one of them and started drinking as he walked up to the cashier.

"You do know that's stealing, right?" the cashier asked Jakari.

He took another swallow of the beer, looking the older Caucasian lady up and down before kissing his teeth. Tonight wasn't the night for him to deal with this type of bullshit.

"I know you see me in line trying to pay for this shit. Always trying to accuse a black man of some bogus ass shit. If I was trying to steal, my black ass would be walking out the door instead of standing here counting all those wrinkles in your face. Take this shit, kiss my ass, and keep the change. You can buy some fucking manners with that shit," Jakari said as he tossed the five-dollar bill on the counter.

All eyes were on him as he stomped to his car. Jakari walked around, thinking that he was someone that the people in the hood looked up to, but in reality, he was just another form of entertainment and something for people to sit around and talk about when he wasn't around. Everyone knew that he had solidified his clown card by doing Diamond wrong and causing her to leave him for good. The bad part about everything is that he wasn't even fucking with another female during the time he neglected to come home. He was chilling with his friends, playing video games and smoking weed. They kept telling him to go home, but he didn't want to hear Diamond's mouth after he stayed out the first night. Time got away from him, and before he knew it the one night turned into two. If it wasn't for his homies constantly telling him to go home before he lost Diamond, he would've stayed at least another night. Now he was riding around town, avoiding going to his mother's to deal with her bullshit. Jakari wished he had at least gotten some head at least from another female since he lost Diamond anyway. He had cheated on her before, and Diamond forgave him. The irony of the fact that the one time he didn't cheat, he lost her for good wasn't funny to Jakari.

By the time he finished the last beer, he was having a problem dealing with his emotions. Here he was, driving around, crying like a woman. Wiping the tears from his face, he decided that he needed to have a sit-down with Legend about Diamond. It was clear that she wasn't being truthful about her involvement with Legend. He knew talking to Legend himself would get him the truth for sure. The amount of the bottom-of-the-barrel malt liquor gave Jakari an unbelievable amount of courage. Jakari pulled up at the last place he knew that Legend would hang out at from time to time. He parked in the front of the club that had a line wrapped around the building. Bypassing the line, he slighted staggered up to the door guy with the clipboard in his hand.

"I need you to go tell Legend to bring his black ass out here!" Jakari yelled, making all conversations cease, gaining the attention of everyone that could hear.

"Bruh, I think you need to sleep that shit off. Coming here looking for Legend is not gonna end well for you, partna. Get the fuck on," the bouncer said.

"Nah, I came to talk to that motherfucker. Go get his ass. I know he's here. I'm trying to see big bad Legend. Go get that nigga, mane," Jakari continued.

Now people had their phones out and were streaming on various social media platforms. Everyone was laughing and commenting how they knew if Legend was there, he would've been outside already. All the way in California, Celeste was on her Instagram page. When she heard the name Legend, she sat up on her bed. She watched as a guy she'd never seen before was standing outside of a club yelling for Legend to bring his ass out of the club. It was too bad that Legend wasn't there because she was sure if Legend was there, he would've been beating the guys ass right now. She had seen times where it took multiple men to pull Legend off someone who had disrespected him in the slightest way. As the man continued to rant and rave, Celeste slipped on her house shoes to rush down the hall to the room that Legend was sleeping in. She banged on the door, hoping that Legend would open the door before the man left the club.

"You're at the wrong door, Celeste. Get the fuck on. You know I don't deal with you like that," Legend said groggily.

He was pissed that she had woken him up only to stand there with a dumbass smirk on her face.

"I don't know how long y'all planned on being here, but it looks like you're needed back home," Celeste said as she held the phone in Legend's face.

Legend was about to lay Celeste out until he heard his name coming from her phone. He took the phone out of her hand and listened to Jakari, Diamond's ex, yell out for him to come out. Walking over to the bedside table, Legend picked his phone up. There were numerous missed calls, messages, and voicemails. He had to have been sleeping hard as hell to not have the phone wake him up. Once he opened the text messages, they were all telling him about Jakari showing his ass outside of the club. It didn't help that he was calling for Legend by name. This was the last form of disrespect that Jakari would ever be able to throw Legend's way. After giving Celeste her phone and slamming the door in her face, he made one phone call.

"I knew you would be calling," the person said on the other end.

"Grab him and take him to the basement. Make sure he doesn't leave. Make that shit look clean," Legend commanded.

"Got it," the person said before ending the call.

Legend slipped on his slides and a shirt. His first move was to find Carlito. He needed the jet to get back home. This was an emergency. This would be the first time he asked about using the jet, even though Carlito has been trying to get him to use it for years. Checking Carlito's room, he found it to be empty. Looking at his watch, it wasn't too late yet. The only other place Carlito could be was the office. Legend could see the light from the cracked office door. He also heard voices. He slowed down because it wasn't like Carlito to have people in the house this late at night unless they were spending the night. He had never heard these voices before.

"We know there's a reason why you're holding everything up, Carlito," the first unfamiliar voice said.

"That's what's wrong with you sons of bitches. You always want shit done on your time. If it can be done without me, by all means, lose my fucking number."

"You're the one that's benefitting here, not us," the second voice said.

"How the fuck am I benefitting? I know you don't mean because of the time you say is hanging over my head. Fuck that time. That's the problem with you arrogant motherfuckers. You walk around, acting like you're helping society or whatever it is that you have to tell yourself to punch that stupid ass clock every fucking day. That badge is what people fear and respect, not the motherfuckers that wear it. There's a difference. Y'all need to understand that."

"If you back out of the agreement, you'll definitely serve every minute of the time you do get. An old man like you can't possibly survive in prison for a month and damn sure not for twenty years. I think you need to think about how you're talking to us right now. Your life can change with one kick of your door, Carlito. Don't make us make good on our threat. We expect you to give us something that we can work with, or we'll have to explore other avenues," one of them said.

"Get the fuck out of my house. Don't come back here unannounced, or your ass will be standing on the fucking porch," Carlito told the men.

Legend hurried to the kitchen. He needed to see who the two agents were so he could notice them if they ever ran across each other again. As he moved around the kitchen pointlessly, his mind wondered about what the hell was really going on. It sounded like Carlito was trying to pull out of the deal. If he was, what was his reason? Legend had more questions than answers. He knew they were supposed to play shit calm, but Legend was done with playing the shit nice. Carlito came into the kitchen dressed in his robe. Carlito loved walking around the house in his plush robe, designer bedroom shoes, and an unlit cigar in his hand.

"You love walking around looking like the stereotypical kingpin," Legend joked.

Carlito didn't laugh at the joke. He knew that Legend definitely saw the agents leave. If he did, then he more than likely heard what they were talking about as well. The game was over. It was time for them to have a serious conversation.

"Did you see the men that just left here?" Carlito asked.

"Yeah. I saw them."

"I need you to hear me out before you start with the questions. Last year, I got a knock on the door. There were two agents that the female that Celeste cut behind Justin had called, telling them all types of information 'bout Celeste and her 'Scarface-like' uncle. I don't know where she had gotten all this information from, but she told them all types of shit. Instead of going just off her word, they started watching Celeste and I. They had pieced together most of the details behind my dealings. The one thing that they didn't know was that I've been diagnosed with stage-four prostate cancer. No one knows but me, the doctor, and the doctor's staff, and now you know."

"And me, so finish talking," Justin spoke, alerting both men of his presence.

"It's good that you're here. That means I won't have to repeat myself. Anyway, I was told by the doctor that I had less than a year to live. When they came knocking at the door, I was sure that I was going to check out before they had enough information to do anything with. Leave it up to me to still be here months after the check-out date I got. Having this meeting was my way of letting you guys know that I fucked up, sending those agents on a wild goose chase by telling them that you were the head of everything. You see, I know that there's no evidence of that, no matter how hard they look. I taught y'all very well. Don't think I haven't noticed how unsurprised you both look right now. You both knowing before you got here never crossed my mind, but it should've."

"I heard some of what you told them. It sounds like you're trying to pull out. They're not going to let you."

"They don't have to let me do a damn thing. I have this all under control. If they want you two, they're gonna have to find another way to get y'all because it's not gonna be with me telling them shit."

"What if they know you're stalling them out?" Justin asked.

"Let me worry about that. What are you two doing up? I thought you were both sleep after the flight and all that mess with Celeste," Carlito said.

"I don't mean any harm, but I can't sleep with her under the same roof. She'll fuck around and be standing over my bed naked or some shit when I wake up."

Everyone thought Justin was over the top or always joking, but right now, he was very serious. There was no way he was going to be sleeping or not paying attention when Celeste was around. Carlito and Legend chuckled at how serious Justin looked right now.

"I know the time may come where she will show you exactly who she is once again, Justin. If and when that happens, you can handle that situation how you see fit. I've repeatedly told her not to take things too far when it comes to you and her having or not having a relationship. She can't seem to control herself when it comes to you. I'm sure once I'm no longer here, she'll push you again. I can't promise that she won't push too far. At the same time, I can't tell you how to react to whatever it is that she does."

"Yo, Carlito, hold up. Are you telling me that I can off her crazy ass if I have to?" Justin asked.

There had to be something wrong with his hearing. Did he

just get the green light from Carlito in real life? Carlito got up, walking away from both of them. He had said everything that needed to be said.

“Carlito, wait a minute. I forgot to ask you can we use the jet to fly back home in the morning. Something came up, and we need to get home like as fast as I can,” Legend said, causing a confused look from Justin. “I'll tell you about it later, but we gotta go as soon as we can.”

“Okay. I'll send you the number to the pilot,” Carlito answered without looking back in their direction.

# 12

Celeste was in her room flipping through a bridal magazine. Yes, she heard what Justin said about them not getting married, but she wasn't going to stop trying to change his mind. There's no way that she was going to give up Justin without a fight. Just thinking about his six-foot-one stature decorated with tattoos, there weren't many, just enough to set Celeste's body on fire, but she wanted him inside her again. Her body was heating up when her room door flew open. Seeing Justin's wild hair all over his head falling around his shoulders and upper back, his light-brown eyes had an unfamiliar look in them.

"What's wrong?" she asked Justin.

"I was wrong about all of this," he said, making her heart drop to her feet.

"What are you talking about?"

"You know what I'm talking about, Celeste. Stop with the games. Since you need me to spell it out for you, I'm talking about us reconnecting. I'm not going to be able to do that. This shit is a wrap. My bad for even calling you about it when I wasn't sure in the first place."

"We can talk about this more in the morning when you have a clear head."

"We're flying out tonight, and there ain't shit for us to talk about. Go back to whatever it was that you were doing before I called."

Celeste was so pissed up that she hopped up. Stomping over to Justin, she slapped him in the face. Justin looked at Celeste in a way that caused her to step back in fear. Turning his head quickly in her direction, she could hear the bones in his neck popping. Her faced balled up due to how painful it sounded. Justin's brown skin appeared to darken two shades. Celeste was thinking of the words to apologize, but she didn't find the words before feeling Justin's large hand around her neck.

"If you ever put your hands on me again, I will kill you. Make no mistake about it. I will kill you, then send flowers to the funeral with a card offering my condolences."

Celeste grabbed at his hand with both of hers, seeing life flash before her eyes she attempted to talk, but she only sounded like a crazy person because of how choppy her words came out. Justin waited until her face started to change from the regular tan she always had. She hit the floor hard enough for everyone in the house could hear and grow concerned. Legend was the first one to the open the room door to what was going on.

"What the hell? I know y'all aren't in here fighting."

"He beat my ass, Legend. I can't believe he did that to me. I thought he loved me," Celeste cried.

"I didn't beat her ass... yet. Since she says I did, I might as well do it."

Legend stepped into Justin's path, stopping him from getting to Celeste. He didn't need anything prolonging their stay in California. If Justin got his hands on her, they would have to stay in order to get Justin out of jail.

"Why are y'all making all this noise in my house?" Carlito asked.

"Uncle Carlito, Justin is trying to break up with me again. He can't do that after he agreed that we were going to try our relationship again. I admit I got a little upset, and I slapped him," Celeste confessed.

"Celeste, I love you, but I've told you time and time again to let people go that want to walk out of your life. There's no reason that can justify you putting your hands on him. Especially when if you would've kept your spoiled attitude in check by not slicing some woman's face, he might still talk to you. Everything you're dealing with is the result of your actions. No one else's."

"How can you say that when he's the one that was playing with my emotions? He made it seem like we were together when we weren't. You can't misrepresent yourself to people like that, then get mad when they don't react the way you want them to. It should've been discussed that he wanted to date other people."

"We weren't fucking dating! You and I fucked! I didn't date your ass then, and I'm not going to marry you! You thought I was going to try to save face in front of your uncle! News flash, your uncle knows your ass needs mental help too!"

Legend pulled Justin out of the room. If Justin stayed in the room any longer, he would kill her. Knowing his best friend was at his wit's end with Celeste and her shit, instead of taking him to his room, Legend chose to get Justin out of the house period. It was a good thing that Carlito's staff was always on hand and ready to help. There was a driver parked outside the front door, waiting in the car. The driver opened the door for them before walking over to the driver's seat of the Cadillac STS.

"You have to calm down, Justin. I know you're pissed, but what do you expect from Celeste? She's off her meds that she hasn't been prescribed yet," Legend joked.

Justin had to laugh at his friend's toxic sense of humor. Celeste was indeed in need of a mental evaluation. Anyone with eyes could see that. However, Justin was tired of hearing her voice, seeing her face, and just tired of her period. At this point, he expected more from asking a wall to move itself. Although he knows how hardheaded Celeste is, it still pissed him off when she walked around acting like they were in a relationship when he's NEVER told her that they were. The car sped through the night traffic. There were a good amount of cars out, but this was Los Angeles. There were always cars on the roads.

"Have you ever wondered why Carlito never got her any help? I used to wonder about that shit all the time, especially after she cut ol' girl's face. She's a fucking mental patient. That shit is plain as day. He's fucked up for not getting her the help she needs."

"Speaking of that chick she cut, I don't know if you heard all that Carlito said. She was the one that contacted the cops in the first place. That's why she's never contacted you or filed any charges on Celeste. I haven't even seen her ass since that shit happened. When's the last time you seen her?"

"The last time I spoke or saw her was that time I went to the hospital to see her. That shit was all fucked up because her old ass mama tried to fight my ass. It was my fault that her daughter was in the hospital, so I didn't trip about it. She made it clear that she didn't want to fuck with me after that, so I left her alone." Justin shrugged.

Talking about that night was making him uncomfortable. That was the last and final time he ever underestimated anyone. Celeste had succeeded in changing him but not in the way that she wanted. After that night, no woman could ever get close to him again. Before that night, killing women and children would never have crossed his mind. Now, he was fantasizing about how he would kill Celeste. Even though all she wanted was love from Justin, instead of making him fall in love with her or giving him a reason to like her as a person, she succeeded in making him hate her.

Meanwhile, back at the estate, Carlito was in his office trying to pinpoint when things went wrong with Celeste. She's his only living relative, and he was entertaining getting the gun out of his desk drawer to kill her himself. When his brother was killed fifteen years ago in a mining accident, he didn't hesitate having her come to the States to live with him. His brother Emilie never approved of Carlito's choices in life. Emilie was older and chose to look at how the drugs, along with everything tied to them, destroyed Colombia. Instead, he worked in the gold mines for a company that was owned by the cartel. Carlito always told Emilie that it didn't matter that he was working the mines; he was still working for the cartel. Emilie felt that since he had what was considered to be an honest job, he was morally better than Carlito.

Carlito knew that he had a niece, even though he never met her in person. They would talk on the phone from time to time. He never knew who her mother was, and Emilie never brought her up, so Carlito assumed that they had a bad breakup. A few years after Celeste came to live with him, he started noticing some things that she would do that didn't make sense. Once when she was in high school, she was obsessed with one of her teachers. She would tell him about this man every day. Carlito noticed how her face would light up when she talked about him. He started to get alarmed by how she was acting, so he requested a conference with the teacher. At the conference, Carlito found out that the teacher had requested that Celeste be taken out of his class. According to the teacher, she would disrupt the class by asking inappropriate questions during class discussions. Here it was, she was coming home with a new story about this teacher, but she hadn't been in his class in weeks. That was the first sign that her mind wasn't all there.

After the conference, Carlito signed her up for therapy. Celeste wasn't happy about it, so to show her uncle that there was nothing that a therapist could do for her, she chose not to speak. Every day for three months, she would go to the therapist only to say "good morning", "I'm fine", "goodbye", and "see you next week". After that, he never tried to force therapy on her again. Now, he was seeing that he should've not only forced the therapy on her, but somehow made her talk to the therapist.

She was fine after he switched the school that she went to

until she met Justin. After the first meeting, he started noticing her weird behavior coming back. The week after she was introduced to Justin, Carlito brought her a toy poodle that she named Justice. She took Justice with her everywhere. The times she wasn't able to talk to the dog, she would be sad and pouting until she was with her dog again. When Celeste and Justin started doing whatever it was that they were doing the first time, she sold the dog. Then after things fell apart ,she was back asking her uncle for another dog. Carlito refused to get her another dog. After understanding that he was serious about not getting her another dog, Celeste chose to move to Sacramento. They would talk on the phone, but it seemed that she was going out of her way not to come visit Carlito until now. However, Carlito knew the only thing that brought Celeste back to Los Angeles was Justin. His office door opened. Celeste walked in looking like she was a runway model, even though she had tears in her eyes.

"You can't keep living your life like there's nothing wrong with you. You need to get some help, Celeste. I'm not going to be here one day to help you get out of whatever bullshit you put yourself into."

"Uncle Carlito, we know that if you sign me up for therapy, I'll do what I did the last time and not tell them anything. There's nothing wrong with me. I'm just a woman in love."

"You're in love with a man that doesn't love you. This is the same thing that happened with that teacher back in high school."

"Why do you always bring that up? Mr. Turner only had my classes changed because all the other girls in the class were jealous of the chemistry that we shared. It's hurtful that you think there's something wrong with me. Justin is just scared that I'm gonna act out like I did when I walked up on him and that side bitch he had."

"The term 'side bitch' is only appropriate if the person is willingly in a monogamous relationship with someone other than the side bitch."

"Why does everyone keep throwing that relationship word around like that? I allowed him to enter my body. That meant we were in a relationship," Celeste said angrily.

"People have sex with people they aren't involved with all the time, Celeste."

"They do. I don't. Justin will be the last man that I will give my body to. He may not understand it now, but he will soon enough. All of you will. I promise you that."

Celeste wasn't happy that her uncle wasn't on her side. She only needed someone to understand that she and Justin were destined to be together. The door slammed after Celeste stomped out of it. Carlito could only shake his head. It was a shame because he knew death was coming for him. However, Celeste had no idea that the man she loved unhealthily was going to be the one to take her out of her misery.

# 13

"Are you sure you want to off this nigga? I'm just saying, I get it, but if you hurt him bad enough, he'll be shook enough to stop playing with you," Justin said.

During the plane ride, Legend had filled him in on the bullshit Jakari did in front of the club. Legend had been contemplating his next move during the plane ride. He knew that with all the people live streaming on social media how Jakari was calling him out he would be the prime suspect if anything happened to Jakari. The problem that Jakari had was that Legend didn't care about what the cops thought. He had specifically told him to stay away from Diamond. Jakari ignored him and went to her house. It was bad enough that Legend didn't kill him that night at the restaurant. That was the first time Legend allowed him a pass. After that, he ignored everything that Legend said by going to Diamond's house. That was another pass. The way he was in front of the club calling out bullshit for everyone in the world to see was the last pass Jakari would ever get. There was no way he would get another pass from Legend.

The thing that Carlito loved about Legend was that he was a thinker. He always thought of the multiple outcomes of his actions before deciding on his next move. In the streets, there were many examples of people becoming emotional about one action only to allow their own emotions to dictate how they move. Emotions and streets didn't mix, like oil and water. You couldn't be an emotional gangster or a sensitive scammer, or you wouldn't last long. Legend knew how to separate his emotions—well, he did until he met Diamond. He didn't kill Jakari at the restaurant, because he didn't want to hurt her. He had someone watching her while he was in California, because he didn't want any harm to come to her. Now here he was wondering if she would cry or possibly fall into a depression when she heard of Jakari's death. They may have been broken up and she wasn't feeling Jakari, but death hits different even if you don't love the person anymore.

"He's doing too much. I had no business giving him a pass in the first place. It's my fault that he was walking around like I'm some pussy that he could continue to play with. It's the motherfucking audacity of his black ass, thinking the shit he did was okay."

"Please fasten your seat belts. We've arrived at Martin State Airport. The weather is eighty-seven degrees with the sun shining bright. Once we touch down, please wait for the fasten seat belt sign to go off before you get up to gather your belongings," the pilot said into the intercom.

Legend was happy to finally be home. Once the plane was at a complete stop and the seat belt light went dim, they were on their feet ready to take care of all the things that brought them home early. Legend sent out a text message, letting the men that were sitting with Jakari that he was on his way. They finally made it to the car in the parking lot. Once the bags were in the trunk, they were in the car with Legend driving.

"I can drop you off at the house if you want. I know you have some shit on your mind, so you can skip this one if you want."

"Nah, I ain't skipping shit. I'm in there like swimwear!" Justin yelled as he danced in the passenger's seat.

The basement that Jakari was being held in was located in

the Cherry Hill Homes Housing Development. Like most housing projects, Cherry Hill was a place of complicated people and ways. Legend had the projects on lock for years. Everyone knew that when Legend and Justice pulled up, this was either really good or really bad. Either way, no one talked about what went down in Cherry Hill. That's why Legend had them bring Jakari here. When they pulled up to the building on Fisk Road, as usual, people were out having a good time. As they walked to the building, there were various people speaking to them. Legend got to the door and knocked three times followed by pause, then two more knocks. The door opened. Justin and Legend gave the guy dap as they walked in the house. This particular unit was a two-bedroom. There was no furniture in the apartment besides the kitchen table and bedroom furniture for the young lady whose name the apartment was in. Jakari was sitting in a chair with his hands tied to the back of it. When Jakari saw Legend and Justin walk in he knew that his life was about to come to an end. Although Jakari was terrified, he wasn't going out like a punk.

"I heard you were looking for me. Here I am. What you want with me?" Legend asked.

"I just want you to stay the fuck away from Diamond. You're the only thing standing in the way of us getting together."

"Motherfucker, I ain't the problem. You're the fucking problem. Diamond ain't my ol' lady—well, not yet." Legend laughed.

Jakari started cursing and trying to get out of the chair. That only made everyone in the house laugh.

"I know you're fucking her. She's too good for you."

"Nah. She's just what the doctor ordered. When did we start talking about your thoughts? You were dumb enough to lose her for good. Instead of causing a scene outside of the club, you should be trying to fight yourself with your stupid ass."

"Nigga, fuck you, man, on some real shit. Diamond will always be mine. I'll be fucking her so good, having her holler my name and shit again real quick," Jakari said, trying to under Legend's skin.

"That's why your ass is in this fucking basement in the first place. You don't know shit about respect. It's all good because you're gonna learn today. I told you to leave her alone, so why the hell did you pop up at her house?"

"I just wanted to talk to her. That's all. We were just having a conversation. She was acting like she didn't want to be bothered with me. It's all a front though. She's still in love with me. I'm all that bitch knows."

Legend's left hand connected to Jakari's jaw so fast that he didn't know what the hell was going on. The chair tipped over, causing Jakari's head to hit the floor. Legend brought his foot down onto Jakari's jaw. Everyone in the room heard the sound of Jakari's jaw bones cracking. The pain that he was in caused him to cry as he lay on the floor. The blood started to seep out at a steady pace.

"One of y'all go get me a cigarette," Legend told the guys.

He was handed a lit cigarette by someone in the room. Legend then bent down in front of Jakari with the cigarette in his hand. Jakari saw him and started shaking his head from side to side fast.

"That nigga looks scared as fuck," Justin joked.

"Let's talk about the word respect. The definition of respect is to have regard for a person's feelings, culture, tradition, and wishes. I specifically told you not to bother Diamond again, didn't I?"

"I wasn't bothering her though. We were just talking. That's all."

"What you see as talking, she sees as you bothering her. Since you're not using the eyes that God gave you to the best of your ability, I'm going to see what happens when you can only use one eye." Legend paused stood to his feet before he continued talking. "Y'all pick this motherfucker up. I need someone to hold his head still and one of his eyes open."

"Which eye you want open?" one of the guys said.

"Nigga, do it look like I give a shit about which eye? The motherfucker has two. All I need is one opened wide as it can be. Play eeny meeny miny moe to figure out which one. Just hurry up because I need to get some fucking rest."

Justin shook his head as they watched the guys do what was asked of them. He could see the anger radiating off of Legend, so he knew that things were about to get messy. When the guys had Jakari the way Legend wanted him, he walked over to him. The way Jakari was trying to fight his way out of the hands of the guys holding him still let everyone know that Jakari knew something bad was about to happen. Legend stood in front of him, not saying one word as he took the lit end of the cigarette and pressed it to his exposed eyeball. Jakari cried out in a painful way that made a few of the guys leave the apartment. After keeping the cigarette on his eye for almost three minutes, Legend finally took it off. The next place that the cigarette went was inside of his ear, Legend was trying to get the cigarette deep in Jakari's ear.

"Open his mouth. Pull his tongue out."

When his tongue was being held out of his mouth, Legend took the cigarette and put the lit end out like his tongue was an ashtray. Justin laughed when he realized what Legend had just done.

"Nigga, your ass is fucking mental. See no evil, hear no evil, speak no evil. This shit is fucking priceless. That's why I fuck with you."

The yelling out in pain turned into a low consistent groan. You could look at Jakari and see that he was miserable as hell. Legend looked at the man with no remorse. Jakari has pressed his luck too fucking much. Now he was dealing with the consequences.

"Do we need to give him something for the pain?"

"Nah. Fuck his pain."

The whole room laughed. Everyone in the room knew that

messing with Legend was bad for business. When the posts on social media started circulating, some of them had placed bets on what Legend would do when he got home. None of them thought of Legend burning the man's eyeball with a lit cigarette.

"Is that it? That's all you're gonna do," Justin asked.

Legend rolled his eyes at Justin. He would be the one that wanted to see what else Legend would come up with. Legend walked over to the men that were standing close to Jakari.

"Give me your jack," Legend said with his hand out.

The guy placed the gun in his hand. Legend took the gun, took the safety off the gun, and shot Jakari once in his forehead, then once in the chest. He handed the gun back to the guy, turning to look at Justin.

"Nah, but that's it," he said before walking out of the door. When he got outside, he saw London standing outside close to his car. His kissed his teeth as he walked to the car. "Why the hell are you out here?" Legend asked her.

"I heard you were out here. Every time I call you, it goes to voicemail. I miss you, and I know you miss me," London said as she tried to walk closer to him. Legend backed up so that London couldn't touch him.

"I'm good on you."

"What does that mean? We've been doing this for years, and you've never been good on me before now. What changed?" London asked.

She had been trying to get in contact with Legend for the last three or four days. London even took it up a notch and sent him some naked pictures to try to get him to respond to her. He never responded.

"Man, look, I'm tired as fuck. I haven't answered the phone because I don't want to. I'm not fucking with you on that level."

"Since when?"

"Since I just told your special needs ass. London, go' 'head with the bullshit. We're done. That's all the end of the story."

Legend opened his door, got in the car, started it, and pulled off. He knew that Justin was going to help the fellas make sure that Jakari was only a memory, so he didn't need to wait for him. London stood there, in the middle of the street, wondering what the hell had gotten into Legend.

# 14

Diamond was kicked back on her sofa eating grapes and drinking some wine. This was the last day that she had to relax. Ashera was supposed to be coming over, but she backed out at the last minute. Starting tomorrow, she would be working on Alannah's house seven days a week in order to get it completed by her graduation in three weeks. Everyone thought that interior design was just going to the store picking out things that looked good together. It was so much more. There were times when the pieces or fabrics that best represent the person that would be living in the space were not available in town. There were times when statues and figurines were ordered just to come in broken or completely wrong. Diamond had to relax and decompress her mind before things got crazy on this project.

On top of dealing with the unforeseen delays that were sure to happen, there was Legend. He was a walking, talking, breathing, and sexy distraction for Diamond. She had concluded that he liked to see her nervous, which was how she was every time he came around. There was something about his six-foot-two, tattoo-covered body that set her body on fire. Then there were the times when she was able to see him walk around with his sexy bowed legs. She was trying to control it or even ignore it, but when he came around, she turned into a blubbering idiot that couldn't think straight. There was a knock on her door, which she welcomed. It kept her from going down the road filled with sexual fantasies about Legend Thompson. Taking one more drink of wine, she walked to the door, thinking that it was Ashera coming over to chill like they had planned in the first place. She opened the door, not caring that she had on a sports bra and a pair of brown short shorts with the word delicious on the back.

"I know damn well you weren't... Oh shit... Legend, what the hell are you doing here this time of night?" she asked.

She was nervous as fuck that it was him on her porch and not Ashera. Diamond made a mental note to call Ashera and curse her out. Here she is, practically naked, with a sexy man looking at her like she's his favorite flavor of chicken wings. Legend was happy as hell that the Lord was acting in his favor tonight. To see Diamond standing in front of him in her little getup had his dick on hard. He studied every curve of this beautiful woman. When he noticed that, her nipples were hard under her thin sports bra. His mouth began to get dry, which made him lick his lips.

"Legend, my face is not in my sports bra. Why are you here this time of night?" Diamond asked after she gathered herself.

"I know where your face is. I had to come check on you. You are a woman that lives alone with a dumbass ex-boyfriend that doesn't understand the English language."

Legend invited himself in as he stepped past her.

"Excuse you. I know you're the hood famous gangster Legend and all, but you can't just walk in my house like that. You never know. I might have—"

"Nah, you don't have anyone here but me of course," Legend said, cutting her off as he took a seat on her sofa.

Diamond stood there, looking at him like he was crazy as he took the bowl of grapes and started eating them as if they were his. Legend paid the glare Diamond was throwing him no mind as he took his shoes off. When he put his feet on her coffee table, she'd had enough.

"Nah. We're not doing that here. You need to state your business and go on about your business," she ordered as she pushed his feet off the table.

"Man, go' 'head on with all that. I've had a long ass night and an even longer last couple of days. I just want to chill. You know, watch some movies or some bullshit like that."

"I'm sure you have women that would love to spend time with the infamous Legend. Diamond Jackson is not one of those women. You need to go find them."

"I don't want to be with them, Diamond Jackson. I'm more relaxed with you, believe it or not. We may not know each other on a deep level or no shit like that yet, but we will. I should be able to chill with my new friend for the night, right?"

"Friends are not what we are. I don't think we'll ever be friends. We don't run in the same crowd, so there's no reason for us to even try to do whatever it is that you're trying to do. You can go ahead about your business and leave me be."

"Stop telling me to leave, man. I'm not leaving here tonight. I don't want to be around them other broads, because they all want something from me. You're the only female that I know that doesn't want anything from me. That's what I need right now. I got some bad news on my trip, but I haven't had a chance to really sit down and think about it until now. I just need some time to get my mind right. I can't do it at home, because I don't need Alannah all in my face asking me what's wrong. It doesn't look like you were too busy from the looks of the wine bottle half full and these banging ass grapes. You weren't busy, and you don't have nobody coming over. Why are you acting like you're not happy to see me?" he asked with a smirk.

"I'm sure there's somewhere else you could be than over here antagonizing me. Come on, Legend. Why are you really here?"

"I told you some heavy shit has come to my attention and I

need to get away for a little bit. That's all. I promise. You don't even have to talk to me. The one thing I do ask is that you give me something stronger than this damn wine. That shit isn't gonna do nothing for me but give me a fucking headache in the morning."

Diamond kissed her teeth before going to get the bottle of Remy Martin 1738. When she came back with the bottle and one glass, Legend looked at her like she had lost her mind.

"What?" she asked.

"Where's the other glass? I know I have a lot of shit on my mind, but I'm not an alcoholic. I don't drink alone or by myself unless I'm the only one in the house. I'm staying the night, so I don't have to drive drunk or tipsy. Are you really going to let me drink alone in your house? You're a fucked-up host, Diamond."

"I'm gonna tell you now that trying to get me drunk enough to fuck you isn't going to work."

"Diamond, I thought we already talked about this. You're not ready for all that, but truthfully, I'm not over here trying to be a gigolo or trying to bring out your inner thot. I just need a friend that isn't going to ask a bunch of fucking questions tonight."

"I'm not your friend."

"You keep saying that like it's true." He sat up on the sofa, putting his elbows on his knees as he looked her in the face. "Diamond, you're sitting here with damn near nothing on. I have my shoes off, you brought out your bottle of 1738, and you keep telling me to leave, but you don't mean it. The way I see it, not only are we friends, but you're Pam and I'm Martin. You know I'm right, beady bead."

Legend laughed at his own analysis. Diamond could say that she wasn't his friend all she wanted, but if she sat around dressed like that around people she didn't trust or like, Legend would be giving her the side-eye. Diamond poured her a drink of wine.

"I don't have to drink 1738 to drink with you. You have your preferences, and I have mine. Did you eat before you came over here?"

"Yeah. I picked up a burger and some fries. That shit doesn't give you a headache?"

"Nope. I don't get drunk off it either. It just mellows me out. I don't do well when I get drunk, so I usually don't."

Legend could tell that Diamond was dealing with some things just like he was. It was on his mind to tell her that Jakari wouldn't be around to bother her anymore, but he didn't completely trust that she wouldn't tell someone, so he kept it to himself. She'll find out soon enough. He shook his head as he thought to himself that he just killed her ex and was chilling in her house like he didn't take a life. His reason for killing Jakari had nothing to do with Diamond was what he was trying to convince himself. The constant disrespect was what caused Jakari to die. It had nothing to do with Diamond.

"If you want to talk about whatever it is that you have on your mind, I'm a good listener. I'm just saying, sometimes things work out better when you talk about it out loud. You have to speak things into existence."

"That isn't gonna work this time. I just found out that a man that's a father figure to me has cancer and is dying. He told us that the doctors told him that he only had a few months to live. Evidently, their deadline has passed. It's weird because he didn't want anyone to know. If I wouldn't have seen something that he didn't want me to see, he most likely wouldn't have said anything. It just so happen that he figured it out and told us everything."

"Everything? You mean there's more than him dying?"

"Yeah, I know it sounds crazy, but the cancer isn't the worst part. Shit is wild out here. If I didn't have Justin with me, I probably would've been crying like a little bitch on the plane ride back," Legend said with a chuckle.

"Why did you come back early? I thought you were supposed to be gone for longer than a day."

"Yeah, some shit popped off here that made us come back

early. Everything is handled though, so there's no need to talk about that."

"If the guy means anything to you, maybe you should go back to California to be there for him. It's not easy going through cancer treatments alone. I'm sure your businesses can run themselves while you're gone," Diamond suggested.

"Everything isn't crystal clear like that. I know he's going through some stuff with his treatments and all, but I got the vibe that he just wanted some peace and quiet while we were there. Shit is different for the caliber of man that he is."

"No matter who or what he is, he's still a person with feelings and a heart. He may be trying to act macho, but in reality, he may be in pain and crying out for someone to care and love him through this process," Diamond said compassionately.

Legend drank the last of the liquor that was in his cup, poured another one, then placed the glass on the table, before laughing at Diamond. While Legend laughed at Diamond's words, she was confused as to what could've been so damn funny to him. She was serious about everything that she'd just said.

"You're an asshole. I know people might not tell you that, but you are. Not only are you an asshole, but you're the king of assholes. Now I understand why you don't have a woman that you can call your own. Nobody wants to put up with your shit," Diamond argued.

Legend didn't care for the tone that Diamond was using while talking to him. He had heard a million times how much of an asshole he was or how he had no feelings. However, hearing Diamond say it right now didn't sit right with him. He liked Diamond, but if she kept calling him an asshole, he was going to show her how much of an asshole he could be.

"Do you always invite assholes to your house?"

"I didn't invite you. All I did was answer my door."

"Yeah, you did, with no fucking clothes on. I could've been your asshole ex. Did you want him to see you dressed like that?"

"News flash, he's my ex. He's seen me with absolutely nothing on plenty of times before now."

"So you would open the door dressed like that for a man that you no longer have a connection to?"

"This conversation is pointless. He's my ex. I wouldn't have opened the door if I knew he was the one out there."

"You didn't check the peephole though, so how would you know he was out there in the first place. It's late as fuck, but you thought it was a good idea to not put on a robe before you answered the door."

Legend was getting upset thinking of all the things that could've happened to her if there was someone else at the door like Jakari. It didn't matter to him that Jakari was dead, because Diamond had no idea that he was dead. At this point, he realized that she could be in real danger right now if there was someone other than him at the door. Maybe the liquor was getting to him, but he was on his way to being pissed off about a scenario that he thought up in his head. Legend has never gotten so worked up behind a chick before, especially one that he hadn't touched.

"Oh, so not only are you big bad Legend from the hood, but you're the fucking robe police too? Well, how the hell are ya, Mr. Asshole?"

"Diamond, go' 'head on with that bullshit. You know what the fuck my name is, shorty. If you can't call me by my name, you can call me daddy whenever you're ready to take that step."

Diamond was completely pissed with Legend playing with her. Why the fuck would she call him daddy?

"Motherfuckers like you just act like you can say whatever you want, and no-one can say shit back to you. I'm not like those other chicks. I don't give a shit about the rumors about you or none of that so-called gangster shit that you do out here in these streets. None of that means shit to me. Fuck you and your rep, in my opinion, asshole."

Legend stood to his feet, walking slowly over to where Diamond was sitting on the love seat. He leaned over, placing his hand on each side of her. Their faces were so close that he could slob her down if he wanted to. She was clearly flustered by him being so close to her.

"Can I fuck you, Diamond?"

"Legend, what the hell are you talking about?"

"You just said fuck me right. I think your words were 'fuck you and your rep'. Since you get to throw those words out whenever you feel like it, I can too. If you ever say the words fuck you to me ever again, I don't care if it's twenty years from now, as soon as you say it, I will take my dick out and fuck you so good that you forget that I'm an asshole and you're not my woman. Stop playing with me, Diamond. This is my last time telling you that. Next time, I'm gonna pull my dick out, and you're gonna think your life is over. Find something safe to do, Diamond."

"Can you back up?" Diamond asked nervously.

Instead of backing up like she asked, Legend pressed his lips against Diamond's. He didn't stop there. He even placed his hand at the back of her head to deepen the kiss as his tongue entered her mouth. After he stopped the kiss, he purposely stood in front of her so she could see how hard he was due to that kiss. When her eyes saw what he wanted her to see, they got bigger, which made him laugh.

"You talk a lot of big shit to be scared. It's not even out, and you look shook as fuck right now. Find you something safe to do, Diamond. I'll fuck your life up, and that's not my rep talking."

After he told her what he had to say, he took his seat back on her sofa, kicked his feet up, and poured another drink.

# 15

Celeste was pissed that her uncle had even mentioned the phrase "get some help" to her. In her mind, the only problem was Justin's inability to admit that he was in love with her. When she went to sleep the night before, she thought that maybe by the time she woke up, Justin would've at least called to check on her once he got home. Celeste woke up to no messages from Justin at all. She took it upon herself to call him, only to be heartbroken when she realized that she had been blocked from his phone. There was no way for her to leave a message or to hear his voice. She went to her uncle's office. It was the phone in there that she knew wasn't blocked from Justin's phone. After walking into the office, she made sure she locked the door so her uncle couldn't intrude on her phone call. Taking a seat at her uncle's desk, picking up the phone to call the man she loved beyond all reason made perfect sense to Celeste, even though he said he didn't want to talk to her again. As the phone rang, her heart raced with anticipation of hearing his deep voice on the other end.

"Carlito, are you okay? You never call me from this phone." Celeste stayed quiet although her breathing was clear as day. "Yo, say something, man. This breathing shit is weird as fuck."

"It's me, not my uncle. Why did you block my number from your phone?"

"You know the answer to that. I blocked your ass because I ain't trying to talk to you. Now you're calling me from one of Carlito's numbers is not cool. You know I can't block him, so I'm gonna have to figure some other shit out. On some real shit, I'll block every number known to man if that keeps you from calling me with this dumb shit."

"Justin, we belong together. Everyone knows that."

"Celeste, if you call me again, I'll get on a plane just to slap the shit out of you. You look fine as shit on the outside. All small with your nice-sized tits and shit, but beyond that, you're just a basic, batshit crazy broad. Keep your ass away from me if you want to stay alive, Celeste," Justin said before ending the call.

Celeste stood there with the phone to her face zoned out to the point that she didn't hear the office door open.

"Why did you have my door locked? Also, why would you lock it knowing I have the fucking key? I just don't understand you, Celeste. What were you in here doing anyway?"

Carlito was looking around for something being out of place. He knew she was in here up to no good. This room was the only room that didn't have cameras besides the bathrooms. He had it like this because there were important people and important things that were discussed in here. Confidentiality was the most important thing to Carlito and his guests.

"I was on a phone call," Celeste said as she tried to walk past him. Carlito stopped her in her tracks by grabbing her wrists, turning her to face him.

"Leave Justin alone, Celeste. I'm not going to tell you again. That man is living his life on the east coast. Leave it that way."

Celeste rolled her eyes, snatching her hand away, then walked out of the office. Carlito was pissed because he knew Celeste was up to no good. Picking up his phone he called, Justin.

"What, man?"

"Justin, it's Carlito."

"Oh, you must've found her in your office. I thought blocking her would stop her from calling, but it didn't. She'll live as long as she stays the hell away from me. That includes phone calls, messages, social media shit, I'm talking about all of that. When I hear her voice, it makes me feel all itchy and shit. I think I'm allergic to her crazy ass."

"I think you're right."

"Right about what? I know you're not telling me you can be allergic to a person for real. Damn, man. I hope that shit ain't true," Justin contemplated.

"No. I'm talking about Celeste being crazy. She's got some kind of mental thing going on where she fixates on one person. Wight now you're that person. I've tried to get her help, but Celeste thinks nothing is wrong with her. It doesn't matter if the man shows her that he doesn't care or want to be with her. That only makes her feel like she has to do more to convince the guy to love her the way she loves him. Her actions get more erratic, and the only way to stop her is to move her away from the person without any contact."

"That's what I'm trying to do. Her hardheaded ass isn't having it though. I'm tell you if she pops up around here, I'm putting a bullet in the middle of her forehead."

"I can't say that I blame you. It puts me in a messed-up position because she's my niece, but she's not all there and doesn't want any help. It's out of my hands at this point," Carlito said.

"Nah. You don't say it like that. You're supposed to say it's above me now. You gotta keep up, old man."

"Justin, I'm an old guy; therefore, I talk old."

"True indeed. What are you gonna do about Celeste?"

"I've tried to get her help. I don't know if there's much more I can do."

"Damn, that's some cold shit. Did you tell her that about the cancer?"

"No. You guys know that's all that needs to know."

"I have a question for you. What are you gonna do about the

cartel? We know that you were trying to give us up to the feds, but you never said anything about you making it seem like we were skimming off the top to the other cartels."

"What the fuck are you talking about? I never speak to the other heads about what goes on in my empire. If it's not affecting theirs, then there's no need to discuss anything with them. You know that I tend to keep things in house. I don't know who you got your information from, but that part is untrue. I would suggest you try to find out the reason for the lie and who else they told the lie to. There's no need to cause distrust between the different cartels. We all know causing a war brings more problems than just war."

Justin was sitting there thinking about what angle could his family possibly have for adding that bit of misinformation. He couldn't figure a reason that made any sense.

"I'll try to find out what's going on. How are you feeling?"

"Don't start asking me how I'm feeling every five minutes. I'm still the same Carlito, and I will always be him until I check out. I feel like a weight has been lifted off me since I told you boys what the hell was going on. Let Legend know that he needs to be on the lookout for the agents that I was working with. They seem to have a major beef with Legend, although I don't know what it could be. I don't think I'll be up to talking to him after I take my medicine in a few hours."

"Okay. I'll let him know when I talk to him."

The call ended. Carlito chose to walk around the grounds of the estate. The pressure was on, and he was feeling like the weight of the world was mounting. Even though he made the lie he just told Justin sound believable, he was drowning still. Letting Legend and Justin know about the cancer was only one part of the worries that plagued his mind. The damn feds weren't walking away from the investigation like he thought they would. Even though Carlito had tried every trick in the book to get them to scrap the investigation, them only wanting Legend was what it seemed like to Carlito now. Could they have been playing Carlito while Carlito thought he was playing them?

As Carlito walked, he took the time to acknowledge that he's come a long way from a little barefoot little boy back in Colombia. People that were on the outside were prouder of Carlito than the people that actually knew him. Looking around, he agreed that he was living the life that a lot of people wanted, but at what cost? There weren't any children of his own that he had to pass anything down to. He hadn't found love with a woman that loved him with all the flaws that he had. It wasn't until now that he had realized that although his life may look fulfilling and happy, he was anything but those things. There was nothing that he could think of in his past that he was proud of or didn't regret. It was either karma or the Lord's sense of humor that he was battling cancer, a battle that he couldn't win now in his old age. Carlito has prided himself on doing things that people have always told him that he couldn't do. When he was a little boy, he was told that he could never work for a cartel. When he got old enough, that's exactly what he did. After getting in at the bottom-of-the-barrel of workers for the cartel, he moved up the ranks, regardless of the people around him telling him that he couldn't do that either. Eventually, he was the one at the top of the cartel calling the shots. That's when people around him said he would never do it for long. Carlito had been the head for the past thirty-four years. It wasn't until recently that he had to deal with any legal issues in reference to himself. He's paid for many lawyers, judges, and even city officials to ensure that his workers had access to the best of everything even while they were doing time.

While the other bosses were throwing their weight around, making their people feel less than human, Carlito treated all of his crew like family. In his eyes, they were a family. A family depended on one another when times were bad and good. Whenever you were in need, your family was the first that you are supposed to call. That is exactly how Carlito carried it with his entire empire. It didn't matter if you were the maid or the person that cooked up his dope. When he first found out about the cancer, he wondered how he could be good to so many people and still be dealt a bad hand. That's when he decided that the cancer was his karma for all the tears his mother cried before she died and for the distance between him and his brother. When he first found out what stage he was in, he contemplated not doing the treatments and just letting things happen on their own. However, it was the fact that he hadn't put things in motion for Legend and Justin to take over after his death that made him go through with the treatments. Keeping up with the treatment schedule that lasted a year and three months gave him enough time to tie up his loose ends. Then there was another monkey wrench when the doctor gave him less than a year to live. Carlito and the doctor argued because Carlito didn't understand the point of setting up treatment for a longer period of time than he was expected to be alive. Nonetheless, he argued with the doctor to start the treatments, and that is what helped him live past his life expectancy. Now it was time for Carlito to take his life into his own hands literally. He had decided a few weeks ago that he was going to take his own life if the cancer didn't take it by a specific date. He told no one of his plans, and it would remain that way.

# ☙ 16 ❧

Legend decided to surprise Alannah today by picking her up. She was down to the last week of class, and he couldn't be more proud of her. He waited patiently in the parking lot on East Cold Spring Lane within the campus of Morgan State University. It was time for Alannah to get out of class. He decided to treat her to an early dinner and to have her car picked up to get detailed while they were out. It had been a couple of weeks since they had some brother-sister time. Today was the day he put everything to the side to spend time with his favorite nuisance. He watched as Alannah came out of the building. She had a white guy with her. Seeing a white guy on the campus of a historically black college wasn't as out of the ordinary as one would think. There were a growing number of Caucasian students attending HBCUs on minority scholarships. It was crazy to hear when Legend first heard of it happening, but it was happening more and more across the nation. The fact that they were attending an HBCU, they had firsthand experience into what the black person went through every day. It was crazy because the ones that attended a HBCU often adopted some of the ways, traditions, and cultures of the people their parents were often against.

Legend watched as Alannah and this white guy talked and laughed in a way that was a little too familiar for his taste. He never got involved in who Alannah dated, because he figured she would introduce him to someone who mattered to her. Legend wasn't overly protective of her, but something about their interaction didn't sit right with him. When she noticed that Legend was in the parking lot waiting on her, she was excited and surprised. She wrapped up her conversation with the guy, then jogged over to the car. Legend loved the fact that, although she was legally an adult, he was still a hero in Alannah's eyes. They had the sibling relationship that most siblings wished for. Life may have dealt them a fucked-up hand, but you wouldn't know it.

"What are you doing here? Why didn't you call me to tell me you were coming? Where's my car?" Alannah asked in one breath.

Legend laughed before giving Alannah a kiss on her cheek. She was excited to see him, and that made him excited.

"Put your seat belt on, damn. Can you be any more excited to see your handsome brother right now?" Legend laughed.

"Whatever. Just answer the questions."

"Your car is getting detailed inside and out. That means all the ink pens that you have stuck between the cushions will be found. I didn't call, because I wanted it to be a surprise that we're hanging out for the rest of the day."

"Oh shit. Something's wrong, or it's about to snow. There's no way that you, my brother, took a day off just to hang with lil' sis." Alannah laughed.

Legend started the car, pulling off onto Morgan State Drive to head to the interstate. Alannah went through all of the radio stations, just to end up plugging her aux cord in to find some suitable music.

"Who was the white boy?"

"His name is Ryan, not white boy."

"Who is Ryan to you? Y'all were a little too close to be just classmates."

"We're just two students that go to the same college with the same major. Why do you sound so concerned about it? What if I did start a relationship with him? How would you feel about it?

"Is he Tommy from *Power* white or that crazy ass Joe guy white?"

"What kind of question is that? Joe is a serial killer. Do you think I would be chilling with a serial killer? Come to think of it, Tommy from *Power* isn't much better. You need to stop that mess for real. Furthermore, doesn't Tommy beat women?"

"Nah, he kills women."

"Hold up. You put it in a question like it was either or, and they're both killers. That's a lose-lose comparison right there. Either way, I'm bound to die," Alannah said as she laughed.

Alannah knew that Legend wasn't racist, but he was skeptical of white people. That was only because of the types of interactions that he'd had in the past with white people. Living in Baltimore, which was sixty-two percent black within a population of a little over seven thousand people per mile, Legend couldn't say that all of his interactions with white people or other cultures were always bad. However, they were more bad than good. It took him time to get relaxed around Carlito as a result of his past experiences, but there was one in particular that changed Legend's and Alannah's lives forever.

"I had a dream about her last night. It wasn't a bad dream though. I didn't wake up crying or even upset. This is the first time in a long time that she's come to me in my dreams and I not be all to pieces when I woke up. Legend, I know you don't like talking about them, but acting like they don't exist isn't normal or healthy."

Legend groaned because he knew where this conversation would lead. Talking about their parents was not what Legend had planned for today. He should've known that they were bound to come up. Alannah wasn't as coldhearted as Legend was.

Legend allowed the circumstances around him change who he was. When he was younger, he loved spending time with his father, Martin, who was a mechanic that everyone in the hood came to. Whenever Martin wasn't working on cars, he was spending time with his wife, Marcel, and his children. His family was the apple of his eye, the motivation he needed to get through the day, until the liquor and drugs took its place.

It all started with an accident on the job where Martin hurt his back. In a blink of an eye, he was out of work but not out of bills. There wasn't an instant change from family man to the local drug addict. It was gradual. Things around the house were tense just after the accident. Eventually, Martin drifted from taking medicine when he was in pain to taking medicine to sleep in order to not stay up thinking about how far in debt his family was due to him not working. He couldn't handle sitting in the house having his wife and kids look at him like he was a failure. In reality, they weren't looking at him that way, but that was the way he looked at himself.

Addiction is looked at as a disease, but it's really the final destination of long road of all things being low within the person known as the addict. People may go through tough times all the time and not end up an addict of liquor, drugs, pills, or even work, but for Martin Thompson, the liquor and drugs helped him get through the day. He would get up in the morning and have a double shot of whiskey and a Percocet with his breakfast.

Marcel decided that instead of bringing up his changing ways to Martin, she would rather take a second job to help things stay afloat around the house. Legend was the oldest, so he understood the circumstances of what was happening. He saw that his father was a shell of the man he once was. Marcel was, at one time, the most beautiful woman in the world in Legend's eyes. Now she's looking older and tired, maybe even worn down. The family went on to function as a shell of itself for years until there was a knock on the door one night while Legend was waiting for his mom to come home from her second job. Legend was fourteen when the officers came to the house telling Martin that Marcel had been killed in an accident involving a drunk driver. Legend stood by quietly watching his father fall to the floor crying uncontrollably as the two officers stood by watching. He wondered why they didn't say any kind words or even give Martin a pat on the back in a consoling way. They left shortly after they rocked Martin's world, leaving him on the floor wailing in pain and agony. Legend remembered that he was the one that helped Alannah get ready for bed, read her a bedtime story, and woke her up for school the next morning. It was that day he promised that he would always be the one to take care of Alannah. Martin clearly wasn't capable of taking care of himself or his children. After putting Alannah on the bus for school, he went to talk to Petey about pushing packs for him. Legend wondered what he would've done if Petey would've turned him away instead. When he approached him, there wasn't a backup plan or another way that Legend could make money as fast as he needed to.

"It's not that I'm acting like they didn't exist. Shit, I know that had to at least live because they got together and made us. I don't think constantly talking about them helps anything either."

"Legend, you don't have to be hard with me. We were there together in that house after mom was killed. I know you think that because I was young I don't remember much of it, but I do. I remember a lot of what went on. That's why I go so hard at school. I saw what you had to deal with. All those times you and dad would fight because of him selling food out of the house for his fix. One time you thought I was sleep, but I wasn't I heard it all. Even though I covered my ears, I still heard arguments that turned into you two fighting like strangers instead of father and son," Alannah cried.

Legend never knew that Alannah had seen the actual fight. He knew she was there after the fact but not that she saw it all. It started because once Legend started making money to pay the bills and put food in the house, Martin essentially turned into the son instead of being the father that he was. It didn't take long for word to get around to Martin that Legend was working for Petey. He came home ranting and raving, trying to find out where Legend kept the drugs that he didn't sell for the night. That was one of the more brutal fights that they had. Legend ended up with a cut upper arm while Martin was covered in scrapes, lumps, and bumps. Alannah helped nurse both men back to health. That time was trying for her, but that was when she realized that Legend would go toe to toe with anyone behind her. That was when he became a superhero in her eyes.

"You know that was all behind him getting his next hit. That shit took control of his mind and body. Once he got hooked on it, he never acted like a dad again. Shit, if you want to be honest, I was more of a father than he was, and we all know it. He was a totally different man before the drugs. The shit is sad as fuck how he turned out. I never wanted you to think that seeing him nodding off at the dinner table was normal, because that shit is the fucking opposite of normal."

"Legend, I know the difference from a dope head and a regular person. I was young, not dumb. There were other kids in school whose parents were also on drugs or alcoholics."

This was the first time Legend heard anything about any other kids dealing with the same things at home that he and Alannah had to face. A headache was starting to form for Legend. There's no way that there were other children out here dealing with messed-up households like they did. He rubbed his forehead with his free hand.

"Do you ever think about it?" Alannah asked through her sniffles.

"What are you talking about now?"

"Do you think it's hypocritical that you are on both ends of the drugs? I think about it a lot. You get the profits, even though you know what the families of the drug users are dealing with. The constant fear of their loved one is going to overdose or steal from the wrong person. I know you've had those thoughts just like I have. I still have them now, even after he—well, you know."

"Nah, you want to talk about all this shit, then say it, Alannah. Say what it is. It's suicide. That's what it is!"

"An overdose isn't suicide!"

"When you have a family that is trying to help you or children that you need to live for and you still go out use drugs, it's fucking suicide. He made the choice to keep using. Mom getting killed didn't even make him get right. Nothing could. He was adamant to kill himself, and that's exactly what happened."

Legend pulled into the parking lot of Arundel Mills. Alannah wasn't expecting them to drive thirty minutes out just to hang out. Perhaps it was her persistence of having this heavy conversation with him now that kept him driving. She didn't mean to change the mood between them. It was just that the opportunity presented itself, and she took it. It had been years since she came home to find Martin sprawled across the kitchen floor with dried foam falling out of his mouth. Instead of calling the police, Alannah called Legend, screaming into the phone that "it" had finally happened. When Legend heard the word "it", he knew exactly what she was referring to.

Everyone thought that Legend was coldhearted, disconnected, or maybe even unemotional due to the complicated web of the streets. They were all wrong. The streets had very little to do with who or what Legend is. The life of being an addict's son, an older brother, the protégé to one of the biggest kingpins in North America, the best friend to a hothead, and the son to a wonderful mother that was taken too soon by a drunk driver are all of the things that made him into who he is. All of those things would crush a regular person mentally. However, it drove Legend to be better than all of those people that made him what he was today.

# 17

"We don't have to go in here acting like everything's okay when we both know it's not. I'm not a little girl anymore, and you don't have to keep trying to protect me. It's time that I protect myself. The best way for me to do that is to deal with the past head-on. Avoiding it never helps anything. It only piles it on with all the other shit that I have to deal with day in and day out. I'm sorry for uploading this on you, big brother, but there's never a time where we can just chill and talk about all things, good and bad. You've protected me so much that you don't understand how strong you've made me as a young black woman. I'm not talking about the classes in self-defense or jujitsu. Even on the mental side, you made me strong. I'm able to separate my emotions from any situation because of you. The bad thing about all of this is that you, my big, strong brother, is out here living a shell of a life. You have every material possession that anyone can desire, but you're not happy."

"Alannah, me being happy is not your concern. You're my sister, not my wife. My happiness isn't your concern."

"Why isn't it? If you don't find someone to be happy with, how am I going to spoil my future nieces and nephews? When can I have a talk about you session with my sister-in-law? I need those things in my life. I don't plan on having any mixed babies anytime soon."

"Come on, Alannah. Out of an entire HBCU campus, you end up dating the white guy. That doesn't make sense to me, man."

"Once you get to know him, you'll see that he's a great guy. It hasn't been that hard to hide this from you and nosy ass Justin. I thought it would've been harder. You two have been distracted by whatever, so that gave me free time to move as I pleased. He's even been to the house to pick me up a few times."

"Alannah, you know better than that shit. You don't know shit about this guy."

"What is there to know? He's attending the same college as I am? We've been having a few of the same classes here and there, we came in together, and now we're graduating together. Stop being so paranoid about everybody."

Legend was pissed at how green his sister was acting. She may have been attending some of the same classes as this guy, but Legend sensed something was off about this guy. Time would tell what his true intentions were and if Ryan was going to have to get killed or not.

"You obviously aren't going to believe shit I say right now about Leonardo DiCaprio, so I'll be quiet. I'll even give him a fair chance. I can't speak for Justin, but I'll let him know so he won't scare the guy to death."

"Thank you, Legend. Now what are we going to do about you finding a woman of your own that you can make cute babies with?"

"That's not part of the deal. I'll agree to not avoiding getting to know a woman, but I'm not going to promise you anything. If I find one, then I won't avoid it. That's all I have."

Alannah leaned over, giving Legend a kiss on the cheek. She was happy about him agreeing not to avoid a relationship with someone. That meant that he was open to the idea at least.

"Thank you for at least being open to it. What's dude's whole name anyway?"

"Ryan Lester. He's not from here I think he's from Idaho or Iowa, one of those I states."

Legend nodded his head, not letting on that there was no way a country boy from Idaho or Iowa chose to come to Morgan State University. Even if it was for the scholarship, he could've chose Howard or Morehouse. They were both HBCUs with more flattering reputations and an equally impressive trail of alumni. Hell, he could've gone to Notre Dame, Yale, or Princeton. Legend was sure of it. The more he thought about it the more he felt that there was more off than on with this Ryan guy. How had his day with his sister just added on to his already growing stack of problems?

"Are you ready to shop?" he asked to try to get the day back on track. There was no need to keep questioning Alannah, because she wouldn't have the answers that he needed. It was clear to him that Ryan wasn't who he said he was, but who he really was, was the part that Legend didn't know yet. He was sure that he would find out when the time was right. Today was supposed to be about him and Alannah having a good time, so that's what they were going to do. The last thing he wanted to do was take her happiness away without any proof of what his suspicions were.

"Yes, I'm always ready to spend my brother's money." Alannah laughed as she got out of the car.

There was the smile that was the reason for him being here with her in the first place. They both got out of the car to go into the mall. The only thing on Alannah's mind was shopping while Legend's mind was how to stop the bullshit from hitting him at every angle.

Diamond was finally spending time with her best friend Ashera. They were in a local Applebee's having drinks and appetizers. They both needed this time together to unwind and enjoy each other's company. Ashera had been working her ass off at her job while Diamond had been working on Alannah's house nonstop.

"What are you going to do about Legend when you're done with his sister's house?"

Ashera liked to see the look of excitement on Diamond's face. She had been with Jakari for so long that Diamond had lost pieces of herself. Seeing her smile, laugh, and joke around was a blessing that Ashera has prayed for.

"How did I know you would bring him up? I'm not at work, so why do I have to talk about him?"

"You have to talk about him so I can live my best life through you."

"There is no best life. He hired me to do a job for him, and that's what I'm doing. There's nothing more to it."

"You have to know that he wants you. Play that 'he doesn't want me like that' bullshit with somebody else, I know better."

"I just left Jakari. You can't expect me to jump into anything with Legend like it's the right thing to do. Damn, let my pussy and mind rest for a little bit before you give me to somebody that we don't know."

"You need to get it together. You can't know the man if you don't try to get to know the man," Ashera said as she snapped her fingers.

Diamond and Ashera laughed so loud that the other customers were looking in their direction. They paid the people no as they continued to laugh, joke, eat and drink. When it was time to go, they both visited the bathroom together of course. Diamond was washing her hands while Ashera was still in the stall. She heard the door open, and a nice-looking young lady walked in. The lady made eye contact with Diamond while she dried her hands. A weird feeling overcame Diamond. There was something about the way the lady looked at her. Diamond was trying to remember if she'd seen the lady before, but she hadn't. After drying her hands, she stood by the way waiting for Ashera.

"You need to leave him alone. Some of you bitches don't know how to respect boundaries," the lady said to Diamond.

Diamond looked around the bathroom to see if there was someone else that she could be talking to. When she didn't see anyone else, she realized it was just them two in this part of the bathroom.

"Are you talking to me?" Diamond asked as she pointed to herself.

"I'm not talking to my-damn-self."

"Jakari and I have been broken up for at least a week, maybe even two by now."

"Who?"

"Jakari, my ex-boyfriend. That's who you're showing out for, right?"

"So on top of fucking my man, you're a hoe too?"

"Hold the fuck up. Diamond, is she talking to you?" Ashera said as she came out of the stall.

"You didn't flush the toilet, Ashera," Diamond said.

"I wasn't using the bathroom. I was sending my new boo pussy poses," she answered as she washed her hands. "Now who the fuck are you approaching my best friend behind, Miss Thing?"

"I need her to stay the fuck away from Legend. He's been acting funny since her ass has been in the picture."

"I'm not—"

"I know you better the hell not explain anything to this bitch. If she was his woman, she would know why y'all are around each other so much. This hoe is fucking pathetic and desperate. If you're his woman for real, call him and let him know that you walked up on Diamond," Ashera said.

London looked nervous when Ashera made that suggestion. Her heart started beating fast. She knew she was dead ass wrong for even approaching Diamond in the first place. Now she was put on the spot to call the man that she didn't want to find out what she was doing.

"I would call him, but he's busy at a meeting for one of his companies."

"Diamond, make the call, sis. This bitch needs to be humbled right now because she's doing too fucking much."

Diamond took her phone out to call Legend. The phone rang only two times before he picked up.

"What's the matter, Diamond?" he answered.

"I'm at Applebee's with my best friend, and this female approached me in the bathroom, telling me to stay away from her man."

"Okay, what the fuck are you calling me for? Call ya ex about that dumb shit. I thought you needed some more money for something for the house or something."

"Legend, you're the boyfriend that she's talking about, not Jakari," she told him.

"What do she look like?"

"She's about my height, nice ass body, about a shade darker than me with an earring in her nose and one in both cheeks."

"That's London. She's a chick I used to fuck from time to time."

"Are you sure about that? I'm positive she said that you were her man," Diamond said. She looked at an obviously nervous London.

"Am I on speakerphone? I know that's how you females do when you're trying to catch a nigga in some bullshit."

"Yeah, you are."

"London, we had this conversation the last time I fucked you. I don't know what your goal is by approaching this beautiful, driven, focused, sexy, soft, sweet, and single black queen today, but you know you just fucked up, right? You and I were fucking. Now you're just a bitch I used to fuck."

"Legend, you can't talk to me like this in front of her," London whined.

"Why the fuck can't I? You knew the fucking deal because I remind you every chance I get. I'm not about to be trying to help a grown ass woman understand what the fuck the deal is between us. I'm not a teacher, and unless we're fucking, I ain't ya daddy either. Diamond, take your ass home. It's getting late. London, go live ya life, shorty. If you keep fucking with me, you won't have that motherfucker long," he said before ending the call.

"He just humbled the fuck out of you," Ashera said as she and Diamond walked out of the bathroom.

London stood in the bathroom crying for thirty minutes. She only wanted to get Diamond out of the way. Instead, she ended the relationship she wanted before it could get started. After leaving the Applebee's, London was supposed to go to work. It was only a twist of fate that she saw Ashera and Diamond on their way to the bathroom when she came to pick up her order of food. She cursed herself for not leaving well enough alone by getting her food and going to work. If she would've minded her business, she would still have Legend in her life. Instead of going to work, she chose to go home and sulk. The drive home was filled with thoughts of how she could make up to Legend what she had done. London also had questions about what type of involvement he had with Diamond. The word "house" kept coming to mind. *What house was he talking about? Whose house was it?*

London walked into her house with her purse and food in her hand. She now had a small headache from all the thinking and crying that she'd been doing. She was so bombarded with thoughts that never noticed Legend sitting in the corner of her living room. After he ended the call, he dropped Alannah off and came straight to London's apartment. He watched as she put her purse on the table and took the food to the kitchen.

"This is why I could never make you my woman. You walked in here not even looking around the apartment before closing and locking the door behind you. There aren't any lights on, which isn't a good thing when you live alone, but you like to fuck with people that aren't bothering you."

London was scared to the point that she was frozen where she stood. She had questions in her mind that never made it to her mouth. Any other time, she would be excited or turned on by seeing Legend in her apartment waiting for her. This time, he wasn't there to fuck the shit out of her. He was there to beat her ass. Legend took his gun out as he walked closer to her. London backed up until she was in a corner in the kitchen. He placed the gun under her chin, making her shake with fear.

"Legend, let me explain. I thought that you and her were fucking around," she cried.

"Nah, you and me we were fucking. Me and Diamond are building something strong, something solid. The next time you approach her, I promise I'll kill you, and you won't see it coming. No more chances, London. The next time she tells me something about you talking to her, your last breath will be coming soon after. Enjoy ya lunch. Get some rest. You look tired."

Legend put his gun back in his waistband and left. London looked down to see that she had pissed herself.

# 18

"I keep telling you that you can leave. What happened yesterday was not anything new to me. Well, I guess it was new because I've never been accused of being with someone that I'm not in a relationship with before. There's a first time for everything."

Diamond shrugged her shoulders as she spoke. Legend came to the house an hour after she had gotten there this morning. He'd been with her all day helping when he could, asking questions, and making sure she was okay after being approached by one of his jump offs last night. She told him that she was fine. Truthfully, she was. All the time that she spent with Jakari was filled with more bullshit than a female saying stay away from my man.

"Why did you deal with it for so long?"

"Deal with what?"

"Your ex dude and all his shit. It's not like you're an average chick that has to hold on to the man that makes her feel loved. Diamond, you may not believe it, but you're the shit. You should never settle for a man that doesn't treat you or make you feel like the queen that you are."

"Well, damn, I need to go find ol' girl and have her come ask me about you at least once a month if this makes you act like this."

"I just call shit like I see it. I know there's no need for me to be here as much as I am, but seeing you in your element is sexy as fuck. There are a lot of females that see you as a threat to them. In my eyes, me and you together will be the ultimate boss couple. We're gonna fuck a lot of heads up once we make that move," Legend said as he licked his lips at Diamond.

Diamond was flattered by the way Legend would always make her feel like she was the only woman he saw in the world. It didn't matter that he was always reminding her that they weren't a couple or that they hadn't made love yet. She was still falling for him. The crazy thing was that even with him being an asshole, smart-ass, and thug with a bad reputation, she was still thinking of him and smiling. Her thoughts of him turned sexual at night and more graphic each time. It was a classic case of resisting temptation, and Diamond was enjoying every minute of it.

"You need to go call ol' girl because you're not getting this anytime soon."

"If that's what you need to think to make yourself feel better, you do that. I know that you're gonna give me that for the rest of your life, willingly."

Diamond laughed as she stood on the footstool to hang the drapes properly. Legend went over to help her balance and reach higher than her. The way his body was against hers wasn't helping this no-sex thing that they had going on. Both of their bodies were reacting to the other's being so close. Legend bit his lip while Diamond cleared her throat.

"How's your sister doing?"

Legend let out a little chuckle before he finished helping her with the drapes.

"She's fine. I found out yesterday that she's into white guys," he revealed.

"What's wrong with that?"

"I'm not saying something is wrong with it, but it's just not my cup of tea. I can't see myself with a woman that is anything other than black."

"I guess it's a good thing that you're not the one in her relationship. If he makes her happy, there shouldn't be a problem. Lord knows I wasted enough of my time on a black man that took my heart, body, and soul through the ringer. There were days where I contemplated turning into a lesbian because men weren't doing it for me anymore. I say if she's happy, let her be," Diamond said.

"There's something off about the guy, I can't put my finger on it. I have somebody checking him out. I've always been told to go with your first mind, especially when you meet people"

"What is your mind telling you now about him?"

"That he's hiding something that's gonna hurt her."

"Did you ask him about it?"

"No. I haven't even met him."

"How can you not like someone you've never met?" Diamond couldn't understand what Legend's problem was with Alannah's boyfriend besides the fact that he was white. "I didn't think that you would be racist. That's interesting."

"What the fuck does 'that's interesting' mean? I'm not racist. I just don't trust them white boys enough to be okay with my sister dating them."

"Would you rather her be with a black guy that dogs her out, beats her, or puts her health in danger by being a hoe? Are all of those things cool because it's not a white guy? Why stop at white guys? What about Puerto Ricans? Dominicans? Iranians? Pakistanis? Asians and whatever else? Does she know she's only allowed to date black guys?"

"It's not like that. Why are you making it sound so bad? White people get away with enough shit. They don't need my fucking sister too!" Legend yelled.

Diamond was thrown off by how angry he was getting about

this. There had to be something more going on than just a white and black thing.

"What did white people do to you?" Diamond asked.

"Killed my mother by drunk driving is at the top of the list of why I don't care for white guys," Legend said calmly.

"Are you serious? Hold on... I didn't know anything about all of that. Oh my God. I'm sorry for putting you on the spot like that. If you wanted me to shut up, all you had to do was say it."

"We have to learn how to communicate with each other, so it's all good. I'm gonna tell you now that, even though it may seem like something simple on the surface, there's usually an underlying reason for things that you don't understand. Everything isn't always as it seems. I'll agree to give dude a fair chance, even though I promised Alannah the same thing."

"That's a good start. I don't know what problem you have with him, but just don't bring anything up to her again about it until you have more than a hunch. I'm sure she knows you have her best interest in mind with any advice you give her."

Legend nodded his head in agreement with Diamond. He just hoped whatever it was that was nagging him about Ryan wasn't too bad.

Celeste was supposed to be leaving Carlito's estate since he wasn't on her side with Justin. She felt like he should be helping her instead of taking Justin's side on the matter. She left the house, going to the mall and the club, but ended up at one of her friend's houses for a few days. She let herself into the house to find it quiet, which was out of the ordinary. Carlito was known to have salsa music or the sports channel on TV loud enough for everyone in the house to hear.

"Uncle Carlito, where are you?"

She walked down the hall, noticing that it didn't look like anyone had been to the house since she last left. Celeste went to her room, putting her things down, and called Jorge, one of Carlito's drivers.

"Hola, Celeste."

"Jorge, do you know where everybody is? I just got here, and it looks like nobody's here."

"I don't know. Señor Carlito gave us all two weeks off. He said he was going away and paid us in advance. Have you tried to call him?"

"We weren't seeing eye to eye when I left. If he went away, then I do have the place to myself. I'm going to get some sleep first, I'll call him when I wake up to let him know I'm here."

"Sounds good to me. I'll see you in two weeks, Celeste. Keep an eye on your uncle. He looked a little down when we left."

"I will enjoy your vacation," she said before ending the call.

Celeste took a nice, long hot shower before getting in the bed to get the rest her body desperately needed. It was ten o'clock at night when Celeste woke up. After washing her face, hands, and brushing her teeth, she went to the kitchen to fix something to eat. She decided that now was a great time to call and check on Carlito. When she dialed his number, she also heard a phone ringing in his office. After ending the call, she walked to the office.

"Uncle Carlito, are you in here?" she asked as she knocked on the door. She waited five minutes before she opened the door. Walking in, she saw Carlito's dead body sitting in the chair with his head leaning back, eyes open, and dried foam coming from both corners of his mouth. Celeste screamed at the top of her lungs, then ran over to the body shaking him, as if that would wake him up. She cried as she picked up the phone to call Justin. She prayed that he answered the phone. His number was the only one that she knew by heart. He didn't answer, so she hung up and called him back to back until he picked up.

"Celeste, I know this is your retarded ass. What the fuck do you want? It better be important, or I'm fucking you up."

"I got here a few hours ago. I thought he was gone. All I did was take a nap. That's all I did... He's dead! I can't believe that he's dead!"

Hearing the word "dead" made Justin stop what he was doing. When he stood still, he realized that Celeste was crying hard as hell. Realizing what she was saying, Justin put his head down.

"I'll let Legend know. We'll be there tomorrow on the first available flight. Call the police so they can come get the body and all that shit. Don't call me back."

Justin sat down, wondering how this next phone call was going to go. After fixing two drinks, he dialed Legend's number. There was no way he could tell him this in person. Justin was barely holding it together himself.

"What up?"

Justin tried to get the words out, but he couldn't. Although he heard the words from Celeste, he couldn't make the words come out of his mouth. Tears started rolling down his face.

"Justin, are you on the phone, nigga? What the fuck you call me for if you ain't gon' say nothing? What the hell is up with you? Justin, are you okay? What the fuck you doing?"

"Celeste just called."

Hearing the pain in Justin's voice, he knew what he was trying to say without saying it. Diamond was checking the design app on her phone to see what had to be done next when she heard Legend scream, then she saw his phone fly across the room. She rushed over to him, wondering what could be wrong and what she could do to help. Tossing her phone to the side, she went over to Legend as he was crouched on the floor.

"Oh my goodness... What is going on? Are you okay? Legend, please talk to me. Let me know what I can do," she begged as he began to wail.

Wrapping her arms around him and rocking back and forth was all that she could do as the man she always saw as strong, fierce, scary, and even as her protector was crumbling before her. She still didn't know what was going on that got him to this point, but she knew she wasn't going to leave his side, at least not tonight. She rocked him back and forth until his sobbing slowed and his shoulders stopped shaking. For a few minutes, she thought that maybe he had gone to sleep until he started talking.

"Do you remember me telling you about the guy we went to see in Cali?"

When she heard the question, she pieced together the rest. Diamond squeezed him as tight as she could. They were still on the floor. It was now getting dark outside, and she didn't care about any of that.

"Is there anyone you want me to call? Is there anything that I can do?"

"I know this might be asking too much of you, but can you come to the service with me? I'll pay for everything. I feel like if you're there, it'll be less of a chance of me getting into some shit. You don't know it, but you help calm me down. It sounds crazy, but it's the truth. Whenever you're around, I look for other options instead of fucking niggas up because I don't want you to see that side of me."

Diamond didn't think she had that kind of effect on Legend. She thought back to how he calmed down when Jakari came to their table that first time. He was telling the truth. She just didn't notice it at the time.

"I'll go with you on one condition. My best friend has to come with me," Diamond requested.

"I don't have a problem with that. Hopefully she'll be able to tame my homie. You never know... we might be having a double wedding before you know it."

"Nah, she's not the type to settle down."

"That's what they said about me, but I see that changing soon. Do you have to go home tonight?"

"No. You know it's just me at the house. What do you have in mind?"

"I want you to stay with me tonight. We aren't going to do

anything. I just don't want to be alone, but I don't want to be around anyone that is looking to get anything from me tonight. It sounds crazy as hell for me to say this, but I just want to be close to you."

"If that's what you need, then I'll be there. I can remember you told me that the guy in California meant a lot to you. If me holding you can help you get a grip on life right now, then that's what I'll do. That's what friends are for, right?"

"We're friends, Diamond?"

"Yeah. I think we're friends. I'm just saying, I'm sitting here holding you while you're ugly crying, and I didn't try to get one picture. I have a question though. If I stay with you, where is your sister going to be? I know I'm part of her surprise gift. How is that going to work?"

"You and I will be at the penthouse downtown."

"Oh, fancy-shmancy. Can we walk on the harbor too tonight? The water helps me clear my mind. It may work for you too."

"We can do whatever you want as long as you're by my side."

"If you keep that up, you're gonna be my boyfriend," Diamond said, dragging the word "boyfriend" like the comedian B. Simone.

"Oh, I'm gonna be way past boyfriend status. You need to keep up. Come on. Let's get out of here. All that damn crying has my head hurting like a motherfucker. I don't see how females do all that damn crying. Y'all shit don't hurt afterward?"

Diamond laughed at Legend's question as they both headed out of the door. They may not be an official couple, but for tonight, Diamond was going to take care of her man.

# 19

The ladies were taking their seats on the jet that Legend chartered for the flight to Los Angeles. Justin may have told Celeste that they would be there the next day, but knowing it was going to take time for the funeral arrangements to be finalized, they didn't board a flight to Los Angeles until four days later. They were just flying in for two days—one day for the funeral, and one day for the reading of the will. While Justin and Legend were speaking with the pilot, Ashera took this time to say her piece.

"Bitch, you're in a whole ass relationship."

"Ashera ,what are you talking about?"

"You know damn well what I'm talking about. That damn man has been catering to you since he picked us up from your house. And what the fuck is the deal with Aquaman? Come to think of it, I need to fight you. You should've called me and described his sexy ass to me."

"Ashera, you do know that we are going to a funeral. You do remember me telling you that, right? Ain't nobody thinking about fucking on a trip like this. Go sit your hot pussy ass down somewhere. Anyway, weren't you just sending pussy pics to somebody the other day?"

"Diamond, those were just pictures. He's my boo and all, but we've only been sexting and having FaceTime sex. He hasn't touched, smelled, or seen the pussy in real life yet. Now as for Aquaman, he can see, touch, taste, and smell this pussy before we get to LA if he smiles at me," Ashera said, laughing.

Diamond began to wonder if bringing Ashera with her was a good idea.

"They're both grieving, and all you can think about is sex. That's a damn shame," Diamond fussed.

"Chile, you better get with the times. I sext, phone, and FaceTime sex with three guys, but I'm not fucking them, so no harm, no foul."

"You're absolutely fine with men walking around with a picture of your pussy in their phone? What if they show their friends that pictures that you're sending?"

Diamond couldn't understand why Ashera was so nonchalant about what she was doing. She had always been the more level-headed of the two, but right now, Diamond was questioning the amount of common sense her friend had. No sane person could be okay with what she was saying.

"I want them to show their friends lowkey."

"Why would you want that?"

"I need their opinion to decide if I'm going to start an Only Fans account or not. If I get enough of them thinking I could make some real money with one, then I'll do it."

"Lord, help my friend. She's lost her way," Diamond joked.

"I know you're not talking and you're about to be the queen of all the illegal shit Legend is into these days. Don't tell me the specifics, because the less I know, the better."

The guys came back from the cockpit. They both were quiet on the ride to the airport, which was understandable. That was the only reason Diamond was happy about bringing Ashera. She may have been crazy, but she was somebody for her to talk to. The entire flight, the girls laughed, talked, joked, and took selfies. Legend was satisfied with his decision to bring her along. She kept his mind off Carlito's death and why was Celeste constantly calling his phone. He hadn't answered and didn't plan on it. The only way he found out the details of the services was Carlito had informed his driver to call Legend if something happened to him. That made it easier on Legend. The less he had to interact with Celeste meant the same for Justin. Today was the first time Justin and Celeste would see each other since the blowup the last time they were at the estate.

"I want to thank both of you for coming with us. It means a lot," Legend said.

"It would mean more if you can get Celeste away from me for good," Justin chimed in.

"Who is Celeste ,and why is she messing with you?" Ashera asked.

Justin and Legend explained the complicated and toxic relationship of Justin and Celeste. Ashera was ready to punch the shit out of Celeste just because she was one of those chicks that didn't know how to let go. There's no reason why any person can't walk away from a relationship if the other person no longer wants it.

"You don't have to go out of your way, but whatever you come up with that will help her get the hint will be beneficial," Justin said.

"Why don't I just be your girlfriend?"

"That's too dangerous. I just told you about her cutting the other chick in the face."

"Oh, all that isn't happening with me. If the bitch wants to play, we can play, baby. I'm from motherfucking Baltimore. That hoe don't want none. Just to let you know, when I find out who the bitch is that got cut, I'm beating her ass too. How the fuck you let somebody come to your town, cut you the fuck up, and leave. That shit is a no in my book," Ashera dramatically stated.

Justin liked how animated Ashera was being, even though she didn't know him that well. Although he remained quiet, he wondered if she was really about that life or just had a lot to say.

Time would tell because it was a guarantee that Celeste was going to act up when she saw them together. They could've been standing beside each other, and she would have a damn problem. He prayed that Ashera at least punched Celeste in the face a couple of times. It didn't matter if they were at the funeral, lawyer's office, or in the damn funeral limousine. If she popped off, she needed to be popped in her damn mouth. After the plane landed and they were all in the car going to the church, Legend took this time to explain to them what type of people they were going to meet.

"I need to explain something to y'all before we get to the church. I need you both to promise me that what I'm about to say doesn't leave this car. I know there are rumors about what we are into. Without going into details, I want to tell y'all that most of the rumors are true. The man's funeral that we're going to was the head of our organization. Since he was the head and now he's dead, the organization has been passed down to Justin and I. I know that you may have questions, and we'll answer them tonight after the service. I also want to give y'all a heads-up that we are going to see the heads of the other organizations at the funeral. All of these men are important and very dangerous. Since y'all are with us, you have nothing to worry about. I just wanted you to know what you're walking into."

"I know this might sound harsh, but how did he die?" Ashera asked.

"I'm guessing it was the cancer. I never asked though. He had just told us that it was terminal, so I figured it was the cancer," Justin answered.

Ashera and Diamond looked at each other with relief.

"Do y'all really think we would bring y'all to a funeral that had the potential of getting nasty? We would never put y'all in danger like that."

"That's great to know," Ashera voiced.

The car pulled up to the church, and everyone took a deep breath. It was showtime. Justin prayed that Celeste would be too broken up to act a damn fool. The driver opened the door, allowing the women to get out first. Once everyone was out, the men took the women's hands as they walked into the service. There were empty seats in front of the church reserved for them. As if all eyes weren't already on them, they had to sit next to Celeste and the estate staff. Celeste could be heard mumbling. Ashera was cool with her doing that as long as the shit wasn't directed at her. They all sat stoically during the service. At the ending of the service, everyone had gathered in front of the church while they waited for the casket to be loaded into the horse and carriage.

"Justin, can I have a word with you while we wait?" Celeste asked.

"He's grieving and not up to talking. I'm sure if he wanted to talk to you, he would've spoke when we first saw you," Ashera answered.

"Who the fuck are you?"

"Just all me Ma Bell because getting through me is the only way you can communicate with him."

"We have history. You should respect it," Celeste replied.

"If I were you, I would recognize that I'm respecting your uncle's funeral. Now we can walk across the street or down the street if you want to have a more in-depth conversation."

"I guess he hasn't told you about me. I'm known to cut bitches."

"Oh, no, he told me all about you. He also told me that you were hard of hearing. I don't care about getting cut. That's what plastic surgeons are for. If I were you I would be concerned for my life while you're out here bragging about cutting people. Where I'm from, if someone cuts you in a fight, the only choice you have to get your lick back is to cut them worse or kill them. Which one do you prefer?" Ashera asked.

Justin was amused with the back-and-forth, but this was not the time of place for it. They were there to honor Carlito's memory. All that other stuff could wait. It didn't matter how bad he wanted to see Celeste get put in her place. If he allowed it to go down now, it would be an embarrassment on Carlito's memory. He rushed Ashera to the limousine, making sure he locked the doors before closing them to keep her in the car. Legend and Diamond walked around, greeting a few people, before going to the limousine themselves. Legend paused when he saw a familiar face out of place. He made sure Diamond was settled in the limousine before going to get Justin. He found Justin talking to someone. He pulled him to the side where no one could hear them.

"Do you see that guy in the gray suit standing by the van?" Legend asked Justin.

"Yeah. What about him?"

"That's Alannah's boyfriend. I knew something wasn't right with him when I saw him. I know she's not going to believe me when I tell her this shit."

"Hold up. That's the fed van. Why the hell is Alannah fucking with a fed?"

"She thinks he's a college student that she has classes with. If he's a fed and they have been going to college together for the last four years, they've been watching us for a lot longer than Carlito said," Legend said as he thought out loud.

"What do you want to do?"

"We gotta take our asses home. This shit ain't adding up."

"What do you want to do about the lawyer's meeting we have tomorrow?"

"We're gonna have to reschedule it. We have more important shit to deal with."

"I'll make the call. Let's get the fuck out of here. I'm starting to hate Los Angeles," Justin said as they headed back to the car.

## 20

"Well, that's not good," Agent Lester said as he watched Justin and Legend rush to the car.

"I told you to stay in Baltimore. He's going to tell his sister that he saw you here. Do you even have a foundation for the lie you're going to have to tell to stay on her good side?" Agent Johnson asked.

"I didn't think that he would see me with all the people over there."

"Just like you didn't think it was weird for a white boy to attend an HBCU in fucking Baltimore! If you fuck up this investigation, it'll be your ass on a platter. Do you understand me? I suggest you get your ass back to Baltimore because the shit is about to hit the fan," Agent Johnson ordered.

"What if we do something to take his mind off seeing me?"

"What the fuck is that supposed to be? He's probably calling his sister now. I don't even know why I'm listening to any of your suggestions. What is your bright idea?"

Agent Lester smiled as if he had the best idea in the world.

"We grab the girlfriend. If he's busy trying to find her. He'll forget all about seeing me. It's a win-win situation. We get to rattle the girlfriend so she can tell us what she knows. Hell, if we scare her good enough, she'll tell us some shit that we don't know," Agent Lester said, sounding sure of himself.

"It sounds like it could work," Agent Johnson said.

"What if she doesn't know anything? It's not like she's been around. We've been watching these two for five years. The chick just started coming around. There isn't much that she could know. The other girl has been around him longer, and that bitch didn't know shit," Agent Cannon asked.

"What is it with you, Cannon? We're trying to take these guys down before the agency pulls the investigation all together. Whose side are you on here?" Agent Johnson asked.

"I'm just bringing it to your attention that snatching up that broad is only going to piss him off. If he saw Agent Lester's face, then he knows that we're looking into him. If we do this and it goes south, he's going to be looking for us instead."

"How would he know that we're the ones that took her if we get her to help us bring him down? If she joins us, then we won't have to keep working on the sister. I don't think the sister knows anything anyway. Carlito was the only one that we could confirm knew anything. Everyone else we involve are only possibilities, nothing confirmed or substantial. This investigation is in jeopardy of falling apart before it ever got together. We're running out of time, gentlemen, so we better figure something out, and soon. I say that grabbing the girlfriend is the best chance that we have at anything. If we want to really get her scared, we can say that we know that he helped her start her business and that if we bring that evidence to our superiors, we could have her business taken from her," Agent Lester said.

"That doesn't make any sense if they just met each other. I'm telling y'all that this isn't sounding right. Actually, it's sounding a little desperate. If you go down this road, you're walking a tight rope. If any of this comes out, we could lose our jobs. You both do understand this, don't you?" Agent Cannon said.

"Either way it goes we lose out. At least we have a chance of making something surface if we snatch her up," Agent Lester said.

"If y'all do that, I'll put in for a transfer. There will not be enough charges to stick after he lets it be known that we kidnapped his girlfriend and threatened her. Legend Thompson is not the man you want to piss off that way. He's smart as fuck at what he does, which is why we've been grasping at straws since this investigation started. Let me know now what y'all are going to do. I worked too hard for my career to go down the drain because y'all don't know when to give up," Agent Cannon said.

"I hear everything that you're saying, Agent Cannon. We have to try every avenue before we just let this gangster remain free," Agent Lester said.

"I guess I have to try to expedite my transfer because the shit is definitely going to hit the fan," Agent Cannon said before leaving the van.

Legend was avoiding talking to Alannah for the entire evening and the next day after they came back earlier than expected. He didn't get a picture of her boyfriend, so it would just be his word against the officer's. There wasn't a doubt in Legend's mind that this Ryan guy was using his sister to get information on him, but he was barking up the wrong tree. Alannah had no direct knowledge of anything Legend was into.

Legend wanted to take Diamond to work, but she had insisted that she go alone because she was so backed up. He had some things of his own to take care of as well. It was a long busy day for Legend. His mind was on everything all day. He couldn't focus on one thing to save his life. He had lost track of time and forgot to call someone to pick Diamond up to take her home. He was still in a conference call with Carlito's lawyers when he noticed that it was getting late.

Diamond was finally leaving Alannah's house when there was still some light outside. When she got to her car, there was a weird vibe in the air. She walked faster to her car as she cursed herself for letting everyone leave her there alone once again, even after she promised Legend that she wouldn't. She had been trying to not end up at the house alone at night. Tonight she was so wrapped up in furniture placement that when she looked up, she was the only one left. Just as she was digging in her purse for her phone, she felt a cold piece of metal on her neck. Freezing where she stood, her mouth dropped open.

"I need you to take your hand out of your purse. Drop what you have in your hand."

The voice sounded like it was more mechanical than human. There were so many possibilities of who this person was and why were they approaching her.

"Who are you? What do you want?" Diamond asked shakily.

"I just told you what I wanted. Take your hand out of your purse!"

Diamond did what she was told. Although she was scared to death and wanted to cry, she held her tears. The person took hold of her upper arm forcing her to walk away from her car and the house. She knew there were security cameras that Legend had installed, but she couldn't remember if they were working right now. When they got to the end of the driveway a dark-colored box van sped up, and the side door flew open. The man pushed Diamond so hard that she fell into the doorway of the van. After the rest of her body was forced into the van, a pillow case was placed over her head.

"If he's watching her, we don't have much time left. Get us to the spot quick, Alexander."

Diamond was an ultimate movie buff when she wasn't working. She'd seen the movie *Taken* so many times that she had it memorized. She remembered when Liam Neeson was in the back of the van and the things he did to remember where he'd gone if he ever got away. Diamond repeated the name over and over in her mind so she could at least tell the police the name of one of her kidnappers if she made it out alive. The rest of the ride, which lasted about ten minutes, was quiet. After the van stopped, Diamond heard the door open. She was picked up and placed on someone's shoulder. She started screaming and beating the person on their back. There was so much movement that her pillowcase fell off, the only thing that Diamond saw was concrete. She was trying hard to remember any little thing that she noticed. She was taken in to a room that looked like an interrogation room. When she looked around she noticed the people looking at her wore police badges and guns.

"Are y'all cops?" she asked.

"Ms. Jackson, we need you to try to relax."

"I was just snatched out of a driveway and brought here like I broke some law somewhere. On top of that, I find out that it was fucking cops that snatched me. Do you think telling me to calm down is gonna make this any less stressful?"

Diamond was pissed she couldn't contain her anger. How dare these police officers or whoever they claimed to be handle her like this? She was a law-abiding citizen with not even a parking ticket. There was no need for them to do her like they did.

"Ms. Jackson, we can't take the blame for you being stressed. Maybe if you didn't have a thug for a boyfriend, you wouldn't be in this position. I get tired of seeing all you smart, talented black girls get caught up with these want to be gangsters and end up behind bars."

"Who the hell are you? Nah. Don't answer that, but you can answer this though. Who the fuck is this boyfriend of mine that y'all think I have? Just for the record, I want to say that I'm single and ready to mingle. This boyfriend that's a gangster and a thug is a ghost because I haven't seen him."

All the officers looked at each other, wondering if she was telling the truth or just trying to get out of being questioned. The intel that they got said that she was indeed his new girlfriend. Their informant specifically said they were together. She even had pictures of them together at various places around town.

"Ms. Jackson, allow me to slow things down a little bit. We're agents, not officers. I'm Agent Lester, that one standing by the door is Agent Hawthorne, and the one standing in the corner is Agent Cannon. You were picked up because it came to our attention that you have some information on a known threat to the city. We were told that you and this person are in a relationship."

"I was kidnapped, not picked up. Also, I already told y'all that I don't have a boyfriend. I don't even have any prospects if we're being honest. Now if I'm here to talk about Jakari, he's my ex, and I haven't seen him in almost two weeks."

"Are you sure you haven't been entertaining anyone else?"

"How many times are y'all gonna ask me the same question in a different way? I don't have a boyfriend. Tell me why I'm here, or do I need to call my lawyer?"

"Oh, you think you're a smart one. If you're so smart, why are you sitting here lying to us saying you don't have a boyfriend when anyone can plainly see that you and Mr. Legend Thompson have been spending a lot of time together?" Agent Cannon said as he laid out pictures of Diamond and Legend at various spots around town. Diamond looked at the pictures, then at all the officers and erupted in loud laughter. "What the hell is so funny? This isn't a laughing matter. We can hold you for as long as we want. You may want to stop laughing and start talking," Agent Cannon said angrily.

"I thought y'all only brought people in when you already had the answers to your questions," Diamond said.

"We already know the extent to your relationship with him. You can't bullshit us," Agent Lester said.

Diamond shook her head at the agents as she tried to gather herself enough to tell them that they could go fuck themselves. Once she stopped laughing, she decided to fuck with them since they'd scared her half to death to question her about a man that she was trying to avoid like the plague.

"I do know Legend, but we're not dating."

"We see all these pictures, young lady. You two are doing too much laughing, smiling, and eating in different restaurants. If y'all aren't dating, what the hell are y'all doing? I don't think a man would put money into your little decorating business if he wasn't boinking her," Agent Hawthorne said.

"Legend has absolutely nothing to do with my business. We're at different restaurants having meetings to talk about the progress of me working on his sister's house. I'm not dating Legend. I don't even know him that well. Y'all need to go back to the drawing board because y'all got some bad information."

"How about we use you to find out what we need to bring Mr. Thompson up on charges?"

"I'm not understanding what you're asking me," Diamond said with a concerned look on her face.

"Oh, the smart lady is having a problem understanding. I'll break it down for you. We want you to wear a wire when you're around Mr. Thompson. Let me explain to you how we ended up here before you answer. This man you see here is Carlito. I would tell you his last name, but there's no need, because he's dead. Anyway, Carlito is the one that taught Justin and Legend everything they know about the criminal shit that they do. Once upon a time, we had an agreement with Carlito that he would give us all he knew about Legend so he would have to serve a small amount of time. The thing is, Carlito thought he could play us. He only agreed to work with us because he knew that he was dying of cancer. At the time that we learned that he was dying, we tried to push him to give us the information quicker, but he killed himself. Now we have an incomplete investigation building against Mr. Thompson. Since we were already building a case, we had a list of associates, places that he frequents, and women that he frequents as well," Agent Lester said, pausing to see if Diamond reacted to his comment about other women.

When he saw that she remained unbothered, he continued. “One of those women happily told us that you and Mr. Thompson were now a couple. When we saw all the pictures that she had, along with her own accounts of how he put her to the side just so he could get closer with you, how could we not believe her? Even if you and him are not in a relationship, you are the closest person to him. I have a feeling that if you two aren’t dating now, you will be soon enough.”

“Legend and I have a nice-nasty relationship. I’m the nice one, and he’s the nasty one. I’m talking about nasty as in him being an asshole just to clarify. He isn’t going to tell me shit about anything that doesn’t have anything to do with the work I’m doing at his sister’s house for him. I promise y’all are barking up the wrong tree”

“Well, I can promise you that after we smear the reputation of your business in such a way that you won’t be able to decorate the inside of a grocery store. Now what is it going to be? Are you going to help us bring Legend Thompson down, or are we bringing you down instead?” Agent Lester asked.

TO BE CONTINUED...

www.ingramcontent.com/pod-product-compliance
Ingram Content Group UK Ltd.
Pitfield, Milton Keynes, MK11 3LW, UK
UKHW041823200726
13854UKWH00002BA/520